"Hey! Hey, what's going on? Why's she running?"

Gordon Johnson's question was one Tristan Sinclair could have answered easily—the woman was running because she'd walked into a cabin she'd thought was empty and into a man she didn't know. She was terrified and trying to escape.

He *could* have answered, but he didn't.

If Johnson realized the woman wasn't with Tristan, that she hadn't been invited to their little party, she'd die and the mission would end.

He raced after the woman and yanked her to a stop, praying she wouldn't start screaming. Johnson had a reputation for acting first and thinking later. One bullet, that's all it would take to spill innocent life out onto the rain-soaked earth. Tristan could prevent that from happening if the woman played along.

If she played along.

Books by Shirlee McCoy

Love Inspired Suspense

Die Before Nightfall
Even in the Darkness
When Silence Falls
Little Girl Lost
Valley of Shadows
Stranger in the Shadows
Missing Persons
Lakeview Protector
*The Guardian's Mission

*The Sinclair Brothers

Steeple Hill Trade

Still Waters

SHIRLEE McCOY

has always loved making up stories. As a child, she daydreamed elaborate tales in which she was the heroine—gutsy, strong and invincible. Though she soon grew out of her superhero fantasies, her love for storytelling never diminished. She knew early that she wanted to write inspirational fiction, and began writing her first novel when she was a teenager. Still, it wasn't until her third son was born that she truly began pursuing her dream of being published. Three years later she sold her first book. Now a busy mother of four, Shirlee is a homeschool mom by day and an inspirational author by night. She and her husband and children live in Maryland and share their house with a dog and a guinea pig. You can visit her Web site at www.shirleemccoy.com, or write her at P.O. Box 592, Gambrills, MD 21054.

The
GUARDIAN'S
MISSION

Shirlee McCoy

Steeple
Hill®

Published by Steeple Hill Books™

STEEPLE HILL BOOKS

Steeple
Hill®

ISBN-13: 978-0-373-44301-7
ISBN-10:   0-373-44301-3

THE GUARDIAN'S MISSION

www.SteepleHill.com

Printed in U.S.A.

Enter through the narrow gate. For wide is the gate and broad is the road that leads to destruction, and many enter through it. But small is the gate and narrow the road that leads to life, and only a few find it.

—*Matthew* 7:13–14

To my dear friend Darlene Martha Gabler.
Though we are far apart, you are always
in my thoughts and prayers.

ONE

First-aid kit?

Check.

Water? Protein bars? Check. Check.

Chocolate? More chocolate? Tissues? Triple check.

Not that Martha Gabler was going to need the tissues. She wasn't. She was over her crying jag and done feeling sorry for herself. It was time to move on, to embrace singleness with the same joyful excitement with which she'd embraced being a part of a couple.

The fact that in one year and three months she'd hit the magical age that separated young-enough-to-hope from too-old-to-keep-looking didn't matter at all. So what if women in Lakeview, Virginia, married young? So what if reaching thirty without heading down the aisle was tantamount to walking around town wearing a placard that read Past My Prime?

Did Martha care?

Yes!

She sighed, zipping her backpack and shoving a baseball cap over her unruly curls. She'd come to the mountains to put the past behind her. She didn't plan to spend time dwelling on things that couldn't be changed.

Like her newly single status.

Outside Martha's Jeep, the day was as gray and gloomy as her mood, the deep oranges and brilliant reds of the fall foliage muted in the dreary morning light. Maybe visiting her father's hunting cabin could wait another week, another month. Another year.

No. It couldn't.

She hadn't been to the cabin since she started dating Brian two years ago. Now that he was out of her life, it was time to enjoy the things she'd loved before Brian had pulled her into his high-society world. Time to start fresh, to look with excitement at the new horizons stretching out before her.

Martha snorted and shoved open the Jeep door, stepping out into cool mountain air. Gravel crunched beneath her feet as she hoisted her pack onto her back and turned to survey her surroundings. The old gravel road she'd parked on dead-ended a hundred yards up. Beyond that, a dirt path wound its way up into the mountains. A steep and difficult climb led to the cabin, but Martha didn't mind. Some good hard labor would get her mind off Brian-the-jerk.

She started to close the Jeep door and jumped as her cell phone rang.

Dad.

For a split second she considered ignoring the call, but the thought of seventy-year-old Jesse Gabler hiking up to the cabin was enough to convince her otherwise.

She pressed the phone to her ear, hoping her voice wouldn't give away her emotions. More than anything else, she hated to worry her father, and if he thought she was upset, worried was exactly what he'd be. "I'm fine, Dad."

"Who said that's why I was calling?" Gravelly and gruff, his voice reminded her of all the triumphs and losses they'd faced together since her mother walked out when Martha was five.

"Dad, it's ten o'clock on a Friday morning. Why else would you be calling except to check up on me?"

"Maybe I'm just calling to say hi."

"Right. You can't stand it that I'm going to the cabin alone. Admit it."

"Marti, the cabin has been closed up for two years. It might not be habitable anymore."

"As long as it's still got a roof and four walls, I'll be fine. I don't need more than that."

"Need more for what? Grieving in private over that scumbag doctor? I knew he was no good the minute I met him. Wishy-washy, wimpy kid with a head too big for his scrawny little neck. If I'd had my way you would never have…" His voice trailed off and Marti could almost see his hazel eyes going dark with worry and regret. "Sorry, baby doll. You know how I am."

"Yeah, I know." Which was why she'd had to escape to the mountains. Between her father, her friends, her church and her community, Martha had nearly drowned in the outpouring of sympathy since she'd called off her engagement three days ago. That was the problem with living in a small town. Everyone knew everyone's business. Most of the time, Martha didn't mind, but right now she needed space.

She needed time.

She did *not* need to be smothered by well-meaning people who all claimed to have believed her relationship with Brian was doomed, but who hadn't bothered to tell *her* that.

Her father cleared his throat the way he always did when he wasn't sure what to say, then launched into a safer topic. "It's supposed to storm tonight. You know that, right? The creek might flood its banks. You might get stranded for a few days."

"A few days isn't going to kill me. Besides, I know how to handle myself out here. I was taught by the best."

"Glad to know I taught you something." *Since I obviously didn't teach you how to protect your heart from smooth-talking men.*

Martha could almost hear the words, though her father loved her too much to say them. "You taught me plenty, Dad. So, listen, you take Sue out this weekend, okay? Somewhere fancy."

"Why would I go and do a thing like that?"

"Because tomorrow is the three-year anniversary of your first date and she expects it."

"Three-year anniversary of our first date? Who keeps track of that kind of stuff?" As Martha had hoped, mention of his wife of eight months was enough to distract her father.

"Sue. She's been talking about it nonstop for two weeks. I'd have thought you'd have gotten the hint by now."

"You know I'm no good with hints. You could have given me a heads-up before now."

"Sorry, Dad. I just figured you knew."

"I guess I'd better get to work planning something. You be careful, you hear? And if you're not back by Sunday noon, I'm coming to get you. Love you, baby doll."

"Love you, too, Dad."

She started to shove the phone in her pocket, then thought better of it and tossed it into the glove compartment. Reception was poor in the mountains. Besides, she'd lost three phones in the past two years. A fact her ex-fiancé, Brian McMath, hadn't let her forget.

Not that she was going to think about Brian. Or their relationship. Or why she'd tried so hard to fulfill his definition of what a doctor's future wife should be.

Organized.

Efficient.

Sleek. Slim. Beautiful.

Martha stomped up the gravel road, forcing her mind away from her ex-fiancé. He'd been an arrogant jerk. She'd been too focused on trying to build the kind of family she'd always dreamed of to notice.

Enough said.

Rain began to fall, but she ignored it as she moved up the trail toward the hunting cabin. She *would* put her disastrous relationship with Brian behind her, and she would enjoy her weekend alone. Just Martha and the great outdoors. What could be better?

Forty minutes later, she was thinking there were plenty of things better than walking soaking wet through thick foliage, with chilly air cutting through her jacket and jeans. Panting hard, her heels burning with blisters from new boots, she splashed across a creek and muscled her way up a bank. All the physical exertion should have forced thoughts of Brian out of her mind, but they were still there.

Frustrated, she stomped up the cabin steps, pulled the key from her pocket and swung the door open. The place hadn't been used in a while, and watery light danced on dust motes as she hurried across the room to pull the curtains open. She'd barely touched the thick material, when she heard something behind her. Or maybe felt it. A subtle shifting in the air, a whisper of danger that electrified the room, made the hair on the back of her neck stand on end.

She wasn't alone.

Her heart pounded, her hand froze in place, her mind screamed directions that she couldn't quite follow.

Run!

No! Never run from a predator.

Walk back out the open door. Pretend you don't know someone is here with you. Go. Go, go, go!

Her legs were lead, the pack ten tons of brick as she started toward the door. She'd barely taken a step when the door swung closed, cutting off light, sealing her in. It was like a nightmare, like a horror movie come to life. Dead silence. Pitch-blackness. Someone waiting in the darkness. Her heart thudded as terror pooled in her belly.

Please, God, I don't want to die like some clueless victim in a horror film.

She stepped backward, bumping into something hard, tall. Human.

A scream ripped from her throat, but died abruptly as a hand slammed over her mouth.

"You don't want to do that." The growl rumbled in her ear; a warning, a threat. "Do you?"

Martha shook her head. Anything to get his hand off her mouth and give her another chance to scream. Not that it would do any good. There was no one around to hear. The cabin was miles from civilization.

"Good. Just keep quiet, do what I say and everything will be okay." As he spoke he moved backward, pulling her away from the door and farther into the darkness.

Don't just let yourself be accosted. Fight!

She slammed her elbow into his stomach, but his grip didn't loosen. "That wasn't smart, lady."

Maybe not, but she tried again anyway. This time slamming her foot down on his instep. He grunted, his grip loosening just enough for her to jerk from his hold. She lunged forward, yanking open the door, racing outside and slamming into a short, wiry man.

"Goin' somewhere, darlin'?" His eyes were pale, clear green, his lips thin and tilted up in a sneer. Freckles dotted his face, but they didn't make him look any less like a cold-hearted killer. If death had a look, it was in his gaze. Martha shuddered, stepping back.

"I—"

"Nowhere without me. Right, Sunshine?" A hand dropped onto her shoulder and hard fingers urged her around to face the man who had followed her from the cabin.

Over six feet tall. Light hair. Hard features. Icy blue eyes filled with a message Martha couldn't decipher. He seemed to want her to agree, but Martha had no intention of going anywhere with him or his friend.

"No" was on the tip of her tongue, but before she could say it, the guy behind her spoke. "She's with you?"

"Sure is."

"Buddy won't like it."

"I don't see why he should care, but if it's going to be a problem, maybe I'll take my business elsewhere." He grabbed Martha's hand and pulled her down the porch steps, tension seeping through his palm and into hers. That only added to her anxiety and fear. Whatever was going on couldn't be good, and the sooner she escaped, the better.

"Hey, now wait just a minute." The smaller man hurried up beside Martha, his eyes darting from her to her captor and back again. "I didn't say Buddy would care. I said he might not like it. But that's your problem. My problem is getting you to the meeting place. So let's go."

"Ready, Sunshine?" Her captor cupped Martha's chin, nudging her head up, gently but firmly forcing her to look into his eyes. Silvery-blue eyes that flashed with anger and something else, something softer, but just as fierce. Concern?

Martha blinked. No. That couldn't be right.

"I said, *are you ready?*" There was an edge to his voice, a warning, and Marti nodded because at the moment, she didn't have a choice. Eventually though, she would. And when she did, she'd take it.

Her gaze jumped away from his fierce intensity, landing on the thin man standing a few feet away.

He was still as stone, his empty eyes locked on Martha. Dead eyes. She wasn't sure how she knew that. Maybe some primal instinct kicking in, warning her. Whatever the case, she was sure the guy would kill her in a heartbeat if she gave him a reason. As if he sensed her thoughts, he smiled, his thin lips twisting up into something that should have been friendly but wasn't.

She looked away, meeting the other man's eyes, her heart beating so fast she thought it would leap from her chest. "Where are we going?"

"For a walk. Just relax and enjoy the scenery." He tightened his grip on her hand until it was just short of painful. He clearly didn't plan to let her go, but Martha didn't get the same sense of danger from him that she got from his friend.

She resisted the urge to pull away from his hold and make a run for it. After all, the key to winning a battle didn't lie in acting quickly. It lay in weighing the enemy's strengths, finding his weaknesses and exploiting them. Her father had told her that a hundred times, and she'd rolled her eyes just as many. Now what had seemed like useless information had value. She'd have to thank her father when she saw him again.

If she saw him again.

She shied away from the grim thought and focused her attention on the shorter of the two men. He had a cigarette pack sticking out of his pocket and was panting for breath as he hurried them toward a dirt road. Obviously out of shape, probably smoker's lungs. Martha figured she could beat him in a footrace.

The man holding her hand was another story. Tall, well

muscled, long-legged, he was not even breathing deeply let alone panting. From where Martha was standing, he didn't seem to have any weaknesses. That could be a problem.

She stumbled over a root, rain slashing against her face and stinging her eyes as her captor's grip loosened a fraction, his hand sliding against hers.

Forget about looking for his weakness. Run!

She didn't consider the odds of success. As soon as she regained her footing, she yanked hard, her wet skin slipping from his grip, and ran toward the trees.

TWO

"Hey! What's going on? Why's she running?" Gordon Johnson's question was one Tristan Sinclair could have answered easily—the woman was running because she'd walked into a cabin she'd thought was empty and into a man she didn't know. She was terrified and trying to escape.

He *could* have answered, but he didn't.

Instead, he raced after the woman, determined to regain control of a mission that, until five minutes ago, had seemed ordinary.

Meet Johnson at an abandoned cabin near the base of the mountain. Follow him to an undisclosed location. Bring down one of the biggest illegal weapons rings in the country.

Piece of cake. Or as close to one as any mission like this could be.

So how had things gone so wrong so fast?

Tristan scowled as he closed in on the fleeing woman.

She was fast, dodging around trees and doing her best to evade capture. Still, he managed to catch her easily, snagging the back of her pack and praying she wouldn't start screaming. Johnson had a reputation for acting first and thinking later, and there was no doubt the gunrunner would be carrying a weapon. One bullet, that's all it would take to spill innocent life out onto the rain-soaked earth. Tristan could only prevent that from happening if the woman cooperated. Judging from the expression in her eyes, that wasn't going to happen.

She swung a fist in his direction, and he grabbed it, tugging her so close he could feel her body trembling with fear. He wanted to tell her it was okay, that he was one of the good guys and that he'd make sure she got out of this alive, but Johnson was jogging toward them, and Tristan had no choice but to play the part he'd been perfecting for months.

He gave her a little shake, hoping to convey the urgency of the situation. "What's the deal with trying to run off on me, Sunshine? I thought you were over our little spat."

"Let me go—" She jerked against his hold, and he tightened his grip, afraid he might leave a bruise, but figuring a bruise was better than a bullet.

"I guess you're still mad. Which is too bad, because difficult women aren't my thing. For you, though, I might make an exception."

"You're insane. I don't kn—"

He pressed his lips to hers, cutting off her words in the only way he could think of that wouldn't make Johnson suspicious. Warmth, softness, the sweet scent of chocolate. He inhaled, drinking in the scent, the sound of rain fading, his heart leaping.

Pain shot up his leg as she slammed her foot down on his instep.

Again.

He maintained his grip, but jerked back, staring down into her eyes, surprised by his own reaction to the kiss and to the woman. Johnson was hovering near his back, just waiting to pull his weapon. There was no time for wondering about the woman who was staring up at him. No time for anything but action.

He leaned forward, holding her tight when she would have wrestled out of his grasp, and whispered in her ear, "If you don't want the day to get a whole lot worse, calm down and play along. Otherwise, we'll both be six feet under come daybreak. Understand?"

She didn't, of course. She'd wandered into her worst nightmare and all she'd be thinking about was escape.

Tristan, on the other hand, was thinking about turning potential failure into success. As long as Johnson didn't suspect the truth, the woman would be fine, the mission could continue and nearly a year working undercover and playing a role he had no liking for wouldn't go to waste.

"Do you understand?" He hissed the question into her ear, hoping she'd sense just how important the right answer was.

Maybe she did. Or maybe she was too scared to argue. She nodded, her eyes wide with fear, sandy curls plastered to her cheeks, the baseball cap she wore sodden and dripping. She looked young, vulnerable, scared.

"Good." He kept his voice low so that it barely carried above the rain. "Here's how we're playing it. I'm Sky. You're my girlfriend. Got it?"

She nodded again, her gaze darting toward Johnson who was moving closer, apparently trying to hear their conversation.

"Whatever you say, *Sky*." Her voice shook, but she looked right into his eyes.

"Good," he said, speaking louder for Johnson's benefit. "Like I told you before, we've got this gig this afternoon. The rest of the night is ours." He squeezed her hand, hoping she'd take it as it was meant—a gesture of reassurance.

"You didn't tell me the *gig* would involve hiking in the rain. I came here to have fun. I'm not having fun. I'm going home." She huffed the words, managing to sound irritated and angry rather than scared. As if she really had been out on a lark with him and was annoyed that things weren't going the way she'd expected.

Not only did she seem to be gaining control of her emotions, she also seemed to be trying to take control of the situation. She'd offered a plausible explanation for walking away. Maybe Johnson would believe it and let her leave. "Go, but don't think I'll be calling tonight. I've got better things to do with my time than chase after a fickle woman." Tristan pulled keys from his pocket and tossed them her way, trying to play the part well enough to be convincing.

She caught them, her eyes widening a fraction. "I wasn't planning on waiting by the phone. See you around, Sky."

She pivoted away, the picture of an irritated woman, and Tristan started to believe they'd won this round. She'd return to civilization, report what had happened to the authorities. By that time, the raid would be over and the police would be able to tell her what she'd walked into and how close to death she'd been. Maybe she'd think twice the next time she went hiking through the Blue Ridge Mountains alone.

He should have known things wouldn't be so easy.

"You're not going nowhere. You wanted to come along. You're coming." Johnson moved in close, pulling a gun and pointing it at the woman, then Tristan. He'd use it, too. Kill them both the same way another person might swat a fly.

In other circumstances, Tristan would have tried to disarm him, but these weren't other circumstances. There was an innocent civilian to worry about, and he couldn't take chances with her life. "Cool it with the gun, man. You keep swinging it like that and someone could get hurt."

"Your lady friend keeps causing trouble and someone will."

"I'm not causing trouble. I'm saying I want to go home, but if you're going to get hot about it, I'll tag along with you two instead." She shrugged as if she really didn't care, her movements confident and easy as they started moving again.

Who was she? Not your typical civilian, that was for sure. No panic. No begging or pleading. If Tristan hadn't known better, he would have thought she was a fellow agent. He took a harder look. Short. Pretty. Athletic build. Dressed in jeans, a nylon jacket and hiking boots, she looked like any other weekend camper, but most normal people were tucked inside cozy houses sitting beside blazing fires, not traipsing through the mountains in frigid rain.

Normal?

As if he knew what that was anymore.

Living undercover didn't leave room for normal. It only left room for the job. And right now the job suddenly included the woman trudging along beside him. He kept a firm grip on her arm as they walked. No way could he let her go running off again. Not when he knew Johnson was just waiting for an opportunity to get rid of her. Permanently.

She slipped and nearly went down on her knees, but he managed to tug her up before she landed. "Careful. The leaves are making things dangerous."

She laughed, the sound choking out and cutting off almost before it had begun.

Surprised, Tristan scanned her face. Rainwater slid down smooth cheeks, freckles dotted her pale cheeks, gold and green mixed in the depth of her eyes, soft lips pressed together.

Lips he'd kissed.

Lips that had been softer and warmer than he'd expected.

Whoa! That wasn't the direction his thoughts should be heading. He forced his attention back to the moment, to the mission, to his role. "I'm glad you're keeping your sense of humor, Sunshine. It makes life a lot easier."

"I wouldn't call it humor."

"No?"

"No. I'd call it hysteria, and if I wasn't afraid your friend would pull out his gun and shoot me dead for it, I'd probably be laughing uncontrollably right now."

"You're right to be worried about that. Johnson isn't known for his self-control."

"Maybe if you'd tell me what's going on—"

He pressed a finger to her lips, cutting off her words before she could say something that would get them both in trouble. Johnson might seem oblivious to the conversation, but Tristan knew him well enough to know he didn't miss much. Not when it had to do with the business he was in. The business of death. "Nothing is going on that we haven't already discussed. You need to relax and enjoy the experience."

"Right. Sure. Enjoy it." She wiped rain from her eyes, or maybe those were tears. It was hard to tell with so much water pouring from the sky.

Up ahead, Johnson was shoving through more brush, leading them northwest toward the abandoned logging camp that served as meeting place and auction house for Johnson's boss Buddy Nichols's gunrunning activities. There'd been other auctions before today, other buyers leaving with weapons meant to kill and maim, weapons that even the most sophisticated armor couldn't stop.

Today, though, was going to be different. Johnson might think Tristan was clueless about their destination, but informants had been willing to leak the auction's location to the ATF for a price. A few hours. That's all that stood between the men who were dealing in illegal weapons and justice.

Tristan smiled with grim satisfaction, holding a thorny branch back and motioning for the woman to step past. One gunrunner, one gang leader, one weapon at a time, he was doing what he'd pledged to do after his brother had been shot and almost killed—evening the odds, adding one more good guy to the fight against the bad guys. Now, though, he had something else to think about. Some*one* else. An unknown player in an unpredictable game.

As if she sensed his thoughts, the woman glanced his way, her expression hiding whatever she felt. "How much farther?"

"Not much."

"Which could mean anything." She frowned, wiping at her face again. Rain. Not tears. Tristan was pretty sure of that.

"Which means we'll be there soon. Then this will be over and we'll be out of here." Anything else was unacceptable. Anything else could leave one or both of them dead. "Just keep your head together, Sunshine, and everything will be fine."

"Hurry it up, you two. We've got places to be." Johnson shot a look over his shoulder, his flat eyes settling on the woman.

Tristan didn't like the surge of interest that blazed in his eyes, the flash of heat that brought the only hint of life he'd ever seen into Johnson's gaze.

He dropped his arm across Sunshine's shoulder, praying she wouldn't jerk away and give Johnson something else to speculate on. "Pick up the pace then. We'll keep up."

As Johnson turned away again, Tristan let his arm slip from Sunshine's shoulders, grabbing her hand instead, squeezing gently and silently sealing their partnership. Whether she liked it or not, they were in this together. Lord willing, they'd make it out together, too.

THREE

Martha told herself she shouldn't be comforted by the warm, callused palm pressing against hers, or by the well-muscled arm brushing her shoulder. Somehow though, she was. Which proved just how scared she was. She didn't know Sky, and she didn't trust him.

What she did trust were her instincts, and right now they were telling her that flat-eyed, freckle-faced Johnson was a killer. The gun he'd pulled had been a Glock 22, a weapon so powerful that the bullet would kill her before she had time to realize she was dying.

The thought made her shiver.

She didn't want to die today. She wasn't *going* to die. She had too many things she still wanted to accomplish. That cross-stitch project she'd planned to make for Dad and Sue's anniversary but had never finished. The missions trip to Mexico. The vacation to Australia she'd been dreaming about since she was old enough to have dreams. The ten pounds she wanted to lose so she could fit into flirty little summer dresses.

Not that her size was going to matter when she was lying inside a coffin.

Don't even go there, Marti.
You are not *going to die.*

At least, she hoped she wasn't going to die. Who knew what God's plans were? She sure didn't. Every time she thought she had a handle on what He wanted for her life, He spun her around and started her in a new direction. Case in point—Brian. She'd been so sure he was the one, so certain God had brought them together. Funny how easy it was to believe something was right when you wanted it badly enough. Even funnier how little all of that mattered in light of the fact that she might not survive the next few hours.

Rain continued to fall as they picked their way along an overgrown road, the raindrops like tears that streaked the earth and trees, muddling the colors so that they blended and bled. Probably washing away any evidence that Martha and the two men had passed this way, too. She glanced around, trying to get her bearings, and realized with a start that they were heading toward an abandoned logging camp. She and her dad had hiked this way many times before, even staying overnight in the cabin that had once served as an office. There wasn't much left of the place—a couple of rusted trailers, the cabin. Another half century and the entire place would be overgrown and covered with vegetation.

What kind of business would take place so far from civilization?

What kind of men would be there?

Not the kind of business she wanted to be involved in. Not the kind of men she should be around.

Yet here she was, going where she didn't want to go, with men she shouldn't be with, and she had absolutely no idea how to get out of the situation.

Any time you're ready, Lord, I'm open for suggestions.

She hoped for sudden inspiration, a quick solution to her troubles. She got nothing.

Her fingers itched to unzip her pack and pull out one of her chocolate bars. A little sugar, a little energy and maybe her brain would start functioning and she could figure a way out of the situation. She started to shrug out of the pack, but froze as Sky speared her with a hard stare. "What are you doing?"

Johnson must have heard because he turned, his dead eyes jumping from Martha to Sky and back again. "What's going on?"

Don't panic. Be a ditzy, stupid woman who thought it would be adventurous to wander through the Blue Ridge Mountains with Sky and his friends.

She forced herself to let the pack slide the rest of the way down her arms. "Just thinking I'd have a snack."

"A snack?" Sky's jaw twitched, his blue eyes boring into hers.

She forced strength back into legs that had gone wobbly and did her best to act as if she didn't know how much danger she was in. "Yes. A snack. A girl's got to eat. Right? It's not like you gave me a chance to have lunch before we left."

"Let me give you a hand with that." Johnson yanked the pack from her hands, his eyes gleaming with the hard gaze of a predator and filling Martha with cold dread.

"Knock yourself out."

He rifled through the pack, then thrust it at Sky. "No more stops."

"Or else" hung in the air, unspoken, but Martha heard it clearly enough. She was also pretty sure that if she looked hard enough, she could see the outline of Johnson's gun beneath the lightweight jacket he wore. It would take only seconds for him to pull it, fire it and wash his probably-already-stained-with-blood hands of the situation.

Fear loosened her muscles and joints and made walking almost impossible. Only Sky's firm grip on her hand kept her going. She wanted to go home to her little cottage in the woods, sit on the front porch and watch the sunset behind the mountains one last time; bask in the colors, the feel, the scent of it. Crisp, cool, alive. She wanted to hug her father, tell him she loved him, kiss his leathery cheek just *once* more. Wanted to go out with her girlfriends, have a slice of Doris's apple pie, inhale the scent of laughter, the heady aroma of joy.

Hot tears worked their way down her cheek, mixing with cold rain.

"Chocolate?" Sky's question pulled her away from her maudlin thoughts.

She glanced at the candy bar he was holding out and knew she'd choke if she tried to eat it. "I changed my mind."

"A little energy will do you good." He unwrapped the chocolate, pressed the bar into her hand. "Eat and stop worrying."

To her surprise, he wiped the hot tears from her cheeks, pressing his palm against her chilled flesh, his voice warm as a spring day. "Everything will be okay. I promise."

"Promises are a dime a dozen."

"Not mine. You *will* be okay. There is no other option." He stared into her eyes as if he could pass his confidence to her with a look.

Then the moment was gone. He reached for the candy bar, broke a piece of chocolate off and popped it into his mouth. "Looks like we've reached our destination. Showtime."

With that, he hiked her pack onto his back and pulled her toward the skeletal remains of the logging camp.

Fear was a terrible thing. It made thinking impossible. It made smart people act dumb. And that's exactly what it was doing to Martha. She wanted to yank her hand from Sky's and run, but that would not only be the stupidest decision of her life, it would also be her last. Sky would catch her before she got three feet away if Johnson's bullet hadn't already knocked her to the ground.

The way Martha saw it, she'd done enough stupid things in the past few months to last a lifetime. First she'd dated a guy who had a reputation for being arrogant and thoughtless. Second, she'd continued to date him even after she'd begun to suspect those rumors were true. Third, she'd decided to run and hide rather than face more pity from her friends and family when she'd finally broken things off with the jerk.

Now she was officially done with stupidity.

It was time to be smart. That meant waiting no matter how much she wanted to run. Eventually she'd have a chance to escape. She had to believe that.

Up ahead, thick trees opened into an overgrown field filled with the remnants of a once bustling logging camp. Martha hadn't been there in years, but from what she remembered, things hadn't changed much. The place was just a little older, a little more overgrown, a lot more creepy. Then again, maybe Martha was just more creeped out. To the left, an old trailer sat atop a cinder-block foundation, graffiti bleeding down the side in reds and blues and greens. Stumps and fallen logs stood to one side, skeletons of the life that had once been there.

In the distance, the clapboard cabin where Martha and her father used to stay stood blurry and gray in the pouring rain. Several men moved toward it ahead of Martha and her escorts, their tension filling the clearing and adding to Martha's fear. She didn't much care for the men she'd already met. She definitely didn't want to meet more.

"Maybe I'll wait out here." She tugged against Sky's hold, but he didn't loosen his grip. Nor did he slow his pace. They were heading toward the kind of trouble Martha had never dreamed she would find herself in, and it didn't seem as though there was much she could do about it.

"You'll wait where I tell you to wait. Right in that trailer over there. After me and your friend are finished with business, we'll decide what to do with you." Johnson speared her with a cold, hard glare, his voice chilling in its callousness.

What to do with her? As if she were some disposable thing. Martha's heart raced, her breath came in short, shallow spurts. *This* was terror. Pure and stark and ugly. She forced it back, not wanting Johnson to see just how scared she was. "I'd rather—"

"I don't care what you'd rather. In the trailer. Now."

Johnson pulled his gun, pointed it at her chest.

"Cool it, Johnson." Sky stepped between Martha and the gun, his hand still wrapped around Martha's wrist.

"Do we have a problem?" The words were smooth as honey and cold as ice. A new voice, a new player, another danger. Marti didn't need to see the man to know it, she could hear it in his voice.

"Nothing that isn't being dealt with." Johnson still had his gun out, but his focus had shifted, his eyes on the man who was walking toward them—medium height, well dressed. Power. Wealth. Danger. They oozed off him. It was his eyes, though, that turned Martha's insides to mush. If Johnson's eyes were dead, this guy's eyes were *death.* There was evil there, a blackness that no amount of polish could hide.

He moved toward them, his gaze resting on Martha briefly before he turned his attention to Sky. "You're Sky Davis. We were wondering if you'd show up."

"I got a little sidetracked."

"So I see." Soulless eyes rested on Martha again, and she resisted the urge to look away. "I'm Buddy. You'll have to forgive Johnson's overreaction to your friend. He's very zealous about his job. We've got client confidentiality to protect."

"Understood." Sky spoke before Martha could. Which was for the best as she could think of nothing to say.

"Then maybe next time you won't bring a…friend." He glanced at Martha again. "It makes things complicated."

"She's a member of the Blue Ridge Mountains Militia. I'm teaching her the ropes."

"Not here you're not. She'll have to wait in the trailer. We'll deal with her after we've concluded our business." He nodded toward Johnson who strode forward, grabbing her arm.

"Hold on a minute." Sky pulled her back toward him, and she was sure he was going to protest, come up with some reason they had to stay together.

Instead, he pulled her close, leaning forward, staring into her eyes. "Don't worry, Sunshine. This won't take long."

He pressed his lips to the sensitive flesh behind her ear, his words barely a whisper. "Sorry about this."

Then he kissed her.

Not the bland, almost sterile kind of kiss Brian usually offered. Not a hard, quick kiss to silence her. A searing kiss that burned its way down her spine. A toe-curling, heart-pounding, honest-to-goodness, Prince-Charming-I'm-gonna-love-you-forever–type kiss.

Too bad the guy was a stranger.

Too bad Martha was scared out of her mind.

Too bad.

Because if he wasn't, if she hadn't been, she just might have enjoyed it.

"Mr. Davis." Buddy's voice drawled into the moment, cold and slithery as a snake. "Sorry to interrupt your moment, but we've got business to attend."

Sky released his hold on Martha and she nearly fell.

He didn't give her another look, just walked toward the cabin with Buddy, while Johnson moved closer to Martha, waving the gun toward the trailer. "Let's go."

He grabbed her arm and yanked her forward, nearly dragging her the few yards to the trailer, his grip painfully tight. She didn't complain, though. No way would she give him that power over her. Let him think she was tough, that what he was doing didn't scare her. Let him think that she really was Sky's girlfriend, out for a jaunt and too dense to realize she wasn't going to survive it.

Please, Lord, let him think that.

Because if he did, if they all did, then they wouldn't be expecting her to escape—they wouldn't waste the time and effort guarding her, and she just might have a chance.

Johnson opened the trailer door and shoved her with enough force to send her sprawling on a pile of dirt, trash and other things she'd rather not examine. Before she could right herself, the door slammed shut, cutting off light. A key scraped in a lock, and Martha heard a bolt slide home.

Obviously, Marti wasn't the first to be locked in here. She'd be the last, though, because once she escaped, she was going to the authorities and she was going to shut down whatever illegal activities were going on here.

Her eyes adjusted to the darkness, and she surveyed the room. Trash. Debris. Probably snakes, rats and mice, too. Not her favorite things to share space with, but a lot better than the men outside.

And at least here she wasn't in danger of having a bullet put through her heart.

The thought got her moving across the room to a plywood board that she was sure covered a window. All she had to do was pry it off, slip out the opening and run. She searched the debris for a tool, her mind ticking away the seconds and telling her she was running out of time. Finally, desperate, she wedged her fingernails under the board and pulled. Pain speared through her hands, her nails bending back as the board gave slightly. Blood seeped from the wounds, but she ignored it, shoving her fingers into the wider space she'd created.

"Please, Lord. Please let this work."

She braced her legs, yanking against the plywood with all her strength. It gave with a crack, and she tumbled backward, landing hard on a pile of garbage. Stunned, she lay still for a moment, her pulse racing frantically, demanding that she get up and go. Now. Before someone decided to check on her.

She stood, her thoughts jumping forward, planning a path through the forest that wouldn't be easy to follow, but that would lead her back to her Jeep and her cell phone quickly. She'd call for help while she was driving away.

Her keys!

They were in her backpack. The one with an identification card that listed her name and address. The one that Sky had taken from her. The one that Johnson could just as easily take from him.

This wasn't good. It wasn't good at all.

For a moment she didn't move, just stood frozen in place unsure of what to do.

"Don't be an idiot. Of course you're sure. If you don't get out of here soon, Johnson won't have to use the identification card to find you, because you'll be dead." She muttered the words as she hurried to the window and peered outside.

Rain still poured from the steel-gray sky, the sound masking any noise she might make as she dropped to the ground. For a moment she hesitated, her mind conjuring an image of Sky as he'd looked when he'd stood between Johnson's gun and Martha. Fierce, protective. Heroic. Would he be blamed for Martha's escape? Would he be hurt because of her?

She shook her head, forcing the thoughts away. Sky knew what he was doing, and whatever it was had only become more complicated because of Martha's presence. Without her to worry about, he could easily do whatever it took to survive. She knew it as surely as she knew that staying and waiting for him to return might get them both killed.

She eyed the tufts of overgrown grass that were fifteen feet below, scanned the area, then hoisted herself onto the window ledge.

"Lord, I just need a little head start. Can You help me with that? Because I'm pretty sure that on my own, I'm in big trouble. And while You're at it, could You watch out for Sky, too?" She whispered the prayer as she twisted, grabbed the windowsill and slid out into the rain. Suspended by her throbbing fingers, she took a deep breath and willed herself to drop.

FOUR

Tristan glanced at his watch as Buddy pulled a sleek M16 from a box Johnson handed him and held it up for his audience—a ragtag group of militia men from various organizations around the area. The auction was underway and in two minutes an organized team of law enforcement officials would stream from the woods and take everyone present into custody. It was what Tristan had spent months working toward. Knowing it was about to happen should have filled him with satisfaction. Instead, he was worried. If guns were fired, if bullets flew, Martha Gabler was a sitting duck. The trailer she was in offered about as much protection from Buddy's arsenal of weapons as a sheet of aluminum foil.

He waited until Johnson stepped into a back room to retrieve another case of weapons, then slipped from his position at the back of the crowd and walked out the open cabin door. By the time Johnson realized he was gone, Tristan would have Martha out of the trailer and to safety.

That was the plan anyway. Tristan prayed it would go off without a hitch.

He jogged across the clearing, planning to open the front door of the trailer and hustle Martha out. Before he reached the steps, a muffled scream and quiet splash sounded above the pouring rain.

Apparently the woman he'd dubbed Sunshine hadn't needed his help escaping after all.

Tristan switched directions, racing around the side of the trailer just in time to see Martha struggling to her feet. He didn't give her time to react, just lunged forward, grabbing her arm and tugging her toward the trees. "Next time you attempt an escape, you might want to keep the volume down."

"There isn't going to be a next time, because if I live through this one I'm never leaving my house again." Her teeth chattered on the last word, her face devoid of color.

"You're going to be fine, Sunshine." He'd barely gotten the words out when the world exploded. Gunfire. Shouts. White-hot pain sliced through his upper arm, warm blood seeping down his bicep. Dark figures swarmed from the trees, surrounding them as Martha screamed.

"Freeze! Police! Hands on your head. Down on the ground. Down! Down! Do it now."

Tristan did as he was commanded, pulling Martha with him. Cold, wet earth seeping through his clothes. It was over. Martha was alive. He was alive. God had gotten them both through. The rest was gravy.

An officer frisked him, cuffed him and pulled him to his feet, calling in a request for hospital transport as he eyed the blood seeping down Tristan's arm. Tristan barely heard. He was looking around, searching for something he didn't see. *Someone* he didn't see. Martha stood a few feet away surrounded by uniformed men and women. Her baseball cap gone, her hair plastered against her pale face, mud streaking her cheeks. She must have sensed his gaze, because she met his eyes, tried to smile, but failed.

Tristan wasn't smiling, either.

Something was wrong. Really wrong.

No way had law enforcement started the gunfight. Someone else had pulled a weapon, and Tristan was certain he knew who that someone was. Gordon Johnson had no qualms about shooting a man in the back. No doubt he'd been intent on doing just that. And no doubt he would have been successful if his aim hadn't been ruined by…what? A gunshot wound?

Tristan turned to the police officer. "Who started the gunfight? Your men? Did they shoot someone?"

"We're the ones asking the questions here."

The officer shoved Tristan forward, apparently not knowing Tristan was one of the good guys and not caring that blood was seeping down his arm, or that the bone was most likely broken.

Tristan couldn't say he blamed the guy. The guns being auctioned today were the latest in advanced armor-busting weaponry. The kind that killed cops.

"Look, if the guy who shot me isn't in custody, you'd better make sure you find him. He's Buddy's right-hand man. If he escapes, there's going to be trouble."

The officer stopped walking and turned to Tristan, something flashing in his eyes. Maybe concern. Maybe recognition of Tristan's humanity. Whatever it was, he shrugged. "The guy was coming around the trailer with his gun drawn as we were moving in. Must have seen something that spooked him because he jumped back behind it just as he fired."

"And he's not in custody?"

"Couldn't tell you. Seems to me, though, that you should be a little bit more concerned about yourself and less concerned about your buddy."

"He's not my buddy." Tristan couldn't say more. Not here.

Maintaining cover until he was brought away in handcuffs was part of his job. If the wrong person saw him being chummy with cops, he'd have a difficult time working under-cover again.

"Right." The officer said something to one of the other uniforms, and walked away.

Tristan tried to relax. Tried to tell himself that he'd accomplished his goal—Martha was safe.

He didn't believe it. Not if Johnson had escaped. The man didn't believe in leaving loose ends, and Martha was definitely that.

He grimaced at the thought, blood seeping in warm rivulets into his palm, his head swimming as the officer he'd been left with marched him toward the other handcuffed felons in the center of the clearing.

Officers and agents milled around, relaxed. Smiling. Box after box of weapons were being numbered and photographed. Thousands of dollars' worth of death confiscated. Hundreds of lives saved. The raid had been a success. A huge one.

Tristan should be happy. He wasn't.

It was over, but not over.

The knowledge edged out pain and frustration, his worry throbbing hotly as he was escorted to an ATV and taken to the main road.

It was over. Marti told herself that again and again as she sat in a small room at the Lynchburg Police Department, visions of cold-eyed killers and blood filling her head. Her hands trembled as she lifted the cup of coffee a female officer had brought in forty minutes ago. Forty minutes. It seemed like hours.

She stood, testing her still-shaky legs as she moved to the

door. They held her weight. Barely. Since the moment she'd turned and seen blood seeping from Sky's upper arm, her body seemed to have a mind of its own, her muscles loose, her limbs ungainly. Shaky, unsure, out of sync with her brain. It was like walking in a dream or a nightmare. Only she wasn't asleep.

A soft knock sounded at the door and Martha stepped back as a stocky, dark-haired man strode into the room, his expression neutral. "Ms. Gabler? I'm Officer Miller. Sorry for keeping you waiting."

"It's okay."

"Can I get you something else to drink? A soda? Water?"

"No. Thanks. I'd just like to go home."

"We'll let you go soon. Right now, I need you to tell me what happened this afternoon."

Tell him what happened? Martha wasn't even sure she *knew* what had happened. One minute she'd been stepping into her dad's hunting cabin, the next she'd been running. Guns going off, men shouting. Total chaos. Sky bleeding. She shuddered, taking a seat again. "I just wanted to spend a weekend in the mountains."

She told the rest as quickly as she could, filling in as many details as she remembered until her words ran out and she had nothing more to say. "That's it."

"Great." Officer Miller looked up from the notebook he was scribbling in. "I think that's all I need. Let me just check on a few more things and we'll get you out of here."

"Before you go, I was wondering, is Sky okay?"

"Sky?"

"He was shot in the arm."

"Sky. Right. He should be fine."

"*Should* be fine? How bad was his injury?"

"As far as I know, it's not life threatening."

"But—"

"Ma'am, you've had a long day. I'm sure you're anxious to get home. Give me a few minutes and I'll make sure that happens." He cut her off, closing the notebook and leaving the room, firmly ending the conversation.

Which should have been fine with Martha.

After all, he'd said Sky's injuries weren't life threatening. She didn't need any more information than that. As long as he hadn't died trying to save her, she should be willing to let the matter drop.

She wasn't. She wanted to know more. Was Sky in jail? Was he going to be charged with a felony?

How had a guy who'd willingly risked his life for a stranger ended up a criminal? It took uncommon courage to step between a bullet and another person. It took valor. Heroism. It took the kind of grit most people didn't have.

Sky had it, yet he'd been in the mountains to buy illegal weapons. That's what Martha had been told by police, and she'd seen the evidence of those weapons as officers led her to waiting vehicles. Still, the gunrunning militia member didn't seem to mesh with the courageous hero, and the dichotomy bothered Martha.

She shook her head, forcing her mind away from Sky Davis. Hero or not, he'd committed a crime. He was going to pay for it, and *she* was going to forget him and move on with her life.

She really was.

She was still telling herself that as Officer Miller returned and escorted her outside into the cool gray evening. Her car was still parked in the mountains where she'd left it, so she accepted Miller's offer of a ride. Her only other choice was to call her father or a friend, and either of those options would have involved explaining everything that had happened.

She didn't want to go there again tonight.

Tomorrow, she'd find someone to help her get her car.

Tomorrow, she'd tell everyone about her experience.

Tonight, she'd just pretend that her life hadn't changed. That she hadn't become a different person. A person who suddenly understood her own limitations. Her own mortality.

Dusk tinged the white siding of Martha's story-and-a-half blue-gray Victorian and shadowed the small front porch with darkness as Officer Miller pulled up the dirt driveway. Cute and quaint when the sun was bright, the place looked lonely and old in the twilight.

Martha hesitated as Miller pulled her door open, suddenly not so sure she wanted to be alone.

"You live here by yourself?"

"Yes."

"Maybe I should call someone to come stay with you. A friend? Relative? Boyfriend?" His dark eyes scanned her face, and Martha wondered what he saw. Certainly not the delicate fragility that embodied so many of her female friends. She was more likely to be called tough than vulnerable, strong than weak. Sometimes she thought that was a good thing. She didn't want or need to be taken care of by anyone. Other times, like now, she wished she looked a little more like a delicate rose than a hardy dandelion. Then maybe Officer Miller would have taken the decision out of her hands instead of giving her a choice.

Because, really, there was no choice. Dad had taught her to face her fears head-on, not to rely on others when she could just as easily depend on herself. She'd learned the lesson well. "No, I'll be fine. Thanks for the ride."

"All right. Here's my business card. Call me if you have any questions." He walked her to the door, watching as she lifted the welcome mat and pulled out the spare key.

"Might be best not to leave that there anymore. It's the first place an intruder will look if he's trying to get in."

Twenty-four hours ago, Marti would have scoffed at the idea of someone wanting to break into her modest home. Now, she could imagine it happening; imagine a man skulking in the nearby woods, waiting until the lights went out and then creeping up onto the porch. She shuddered. "I won't."

Her hand shook as she shoved the key into the lock and pushed the door open. Safely inside, she offered Officer Miller a quick wave, then shut the door and locked it again. Maybe she should put the couch in front of it, too. Just for a little added security.

Of course, that would mean she'd also need to block all the windows. And the back door. Maybe even the chimney.

"You are not going to turn paranoid because of what happened. You're *not*."

She spoke out loud as she turned on the table lamps, letting their bright yellow glow chase away some of the shadows. This was her house. Her safe haven. A place she'd bought because of its peaceful ambience and tranquil setting. She wasn't going to let Gordon Johnson or his boss take that away from her.

Tomorrow would be a whole new day. The sun would come up. The sky would lighten, and today's nightmare would fade from memory. Until then, she'd just cling to the knowledge that God was with her, that He hadn't saved her life for nothing. He'd keep her safe. No matter how dark the night, or how dangerous the monsters that lurked in it.

FIVE

The phone rang just after seven Sunday morning, dragging Marti from restless, nightmare-filled sleep. She scowled as the answering machine picked up and Jennifer Gardner's soft southern drawl filled the room. "Marti? Jenny, here. I heard what happened Friday and was calling to see if you needed me to fill in on nursery duty for you. Adam and I just got back from Cancún. It was absolutely the most relaxing, fantastic place to honeymoon. Maybe you and Brian… Oh, I am *so* sorry. I did hear that the two of you broke up." Her pause was dramatic and typical Jennifer. Marti could almost imagine the dark-haired beauty pressing the phone close to her ear, hoping Marti would feel compelled to answer.

She didn't.

She'd spent the previous day fielding calls from friends, acquaintances, local newspaper reporters. She did not plan to add to that by explaining the situation to Jennifer, who, if she'd taken the time to check things out, would have realized that Martha had found someone to replace her in the nursery as soon as she'd decided to spend the weekend in the mountains.

"Marti? Are you there? You do know you're signed up to work in the toddler nursery, don't you?"

"Yes. I know. And, no, I don't need anyone to fill in for me.

Even if I did, I wouldn't ask a lacquer-nailed, overly hair-sprayed former homecoming queen who knows as much about kids as I do about curling irons." Marti muttered the words as she turned down the volume of the answering machine, muting the rest of Jennifer's long message.

Her attitude stunk, and Martha knew it, but she seemed helpless to get a handle on her irritation. Chalk it up to lack of sleep, or too many nightmares. Whatever the case, there was no way she planned to spend another day answering the phone and being nice to people who were more interested in gossip than in her well-being. She was going out. Not just out. She was going to church. At least there most of the people truly cared about how she was doing.

She grabbed a dress from her closet, barely noticing the color or style as she hurried to shower and change. Her ears strained for sounds that didn't belong, her heart pounding a quick, erratic beat. No matter how many times she told herself she was safe, she couldn't seem to shake the fear that had been nipping at her heels all weekend.

When she was a kid, she hadn't been afraid of monsters under the bed or bogeymen in closets. It seemed ironic that she was now. Every noise, every shadow made her jump. Every night was filled with potential danger.

Worse, her hands were still shaking, her pulled-back nails throbbing as she grabbed a brush and raked it through her hair. The pain reminded her of the desperate moments in the trailer; the danger just outside the metal prison she'd been trapped in. Johnson's dead eyes staring at her. Memorizing her.

Her heart leaped at the thought, and she took a deep breath. Johnson was surely in jail now. She would never see him again. The thought should have been comforting, but wasn't. She swept blush across her cheeks, hoping to liven her pale face. It didn't help. She still looked pale. Still looked scared. But she was going to church.

Because there was no way she was going to let fear control her. She smiled at her reflection. There. That was better. All she had to do was pretend she was fine. Eventually, she'd believe it.

She grabbed her purse and Bible. A few hours away from the house would be good for her. Maybe after church she'd visit Sue and Dad, beg a home-cooked meal off them. At least then she wouldn't have to be alone.

Until tonight. When it was dark again and memories of gunshots and blood filled her dreams.

She shuddered, stepping out into cool, crisp air.

"You clean up good, Sunshine." The deep rumble cut through the morning quiet, and Marti whirled toward the speaker. Tall. Light hair. Icy blue eyes that raked her from head to toe. A slight smile curving firm lips. Left arm in a sling that couldn't hide the thick muscles of biceps and shoulders.

"Sky?"

"Actually, it's Tristan. Tristan Sinclair." He moved up the porch stairs, and Marti took a step back, not sure if she should run into the house or stand her ground. He'd saved her life, but he'd also been responsible for dragging her through the mountains with Gordon Johnson. He was a militia member. A man who dealt in illegal weapons. Who hung out with murderers and felons. Who was supposed to be in jail.

"What do you want? Why aren't you in prison?"

"To make sure you're safe, and because I didn't commit a crime."

"You were in the mountains to buy illegal weapons. That's a felony."

"It would be if that's what I had been doing."

"So you're saying you weren't?"

"I'm saying things aren't always what they seem. Now, how about we go inside to discuss this?"

"Anything we need to say can be said out here."

"It can be, but that might not be for the best. You're not safe, Sunshine. The sooner you realize that, the better."

"Is that a threat?" Her heart slammed a quick, hard beat as she reached for the doorknob. He was close, but not so close that she couldn't get inside the house and lock the door before he grabbed her. She hoped.

"It's a warning. Gordon Johnson escaped into the mountains Friday. He still hasn't been apprehended."

Johnson had escaped? A shiver of fear raced up Marti's spine. "Why didn't the police tell me this?"

"You'll have to ask them that."

"I will." The hollow thud of her heart echoed in her ears as she turned and shoved the door open. Of all the men she'd run into Friday, Johnson was the one she most feared. The one whose lifeless eyes haunted her dreams. If he was really out there somewhere, she wanted to know. She'd call Officer Miller. He'd be able to tell her what was going on.

The soft click of the door and the quiet slide of the bolt pulled her from numb fear. Or maybe *dumb* fear was a better term. She'd just let the man who'd kidnapped her walk into her house!

She whirled to face Tristan.

He stood just a few feet away, leaning against the door, blocking her escape. She could run for the back door, but he'd be on her before then.

The phone! Grab the phone and call for help.

She lifted the receiver. "I'm calling the police."

"Good idea. Tell Officer Miller I found your place just fine."

Marti hesitated with the phone halfway to her ear. "You spoke to him?"

"He said you were asking about my injury." He flashed white teeth, but Marti wouldn't exactly call the expression a smile. "He also said you lived off the beaten path at the end of a dead-end street. Not the most secure house in the world. He was right."

He was telling the truth. She knew it. What she didn't know was why he was in her house and not in jail. She hung up the phone. "Who are you? And I don't mean your name."

"Tristan Sinclair. ATF agent. I was working undercover the day we ran into each other."

ATF? It made sense. A sick, crazy kind of sense. "Ran into each other? You kidnapped me and pulled me into the biggest illegal firearms raid in a decade." Something the newscasters had made mention of over and over again as they'd covered the story. Something everyone but Marti seemed to find fascinating.

"I kept you safe until reinforcements could come in and bring you out."

And he'd saved her life. He didn't point that out. Brian would have. He would have been announcing his feat to the world, making appointments with television shows and radio programs, planning a book and movie deal, telling Marti again and again how fortunate she was to have him.

"Sorry if I sounded ungrateful. You saved my life, and I really do appreciate it. Thanks."

"You saved yourself, Sunshine. I just helped a little."

"And got shot doing it. How's your arm?"

"Better."

"Than?"

"Than being dead." He smiled, but Martha didn't think Tristan's potential death was amusing.

"That's not funny."

"No, but I'm celebrating survival, so I'm trying to find a lot to smile about." He smiled again, and some of the tension that had been coiled inside Martha eased. It felt good to be talking to someone who knew what had happened to her and didn't need to ask questions about it. Someone who had shared her experience and could show her how to put it in perspective.

"I guess if you can smile about it, I can, too."

"And you should. You've got a beautiful smile." His gaze dropped to her lips, lingered there for a moment before he met her eyes again.

Her cheeks flamed, her heart jumped, and she resisted the urge to smooth her hair, fidget with her dress. She did not need to look good for Tristan Sinclair. Sure, he'd saved her life, but he was still a man. And men were something she'd decided less than a week ago that she could do without.

She needed to keep that in mind, or she might end up exactly where she didn't want to be—nursing a broken heart and mourning the death of her dreams. Again. It was time to put some distance between herself and Tristan.

"Look, I hate to shove you out, but I've got to be at church in less than thirty minutes."

"Good. Let's go." He took her arm, started walking toward the door.

That was easy. A lot easier than Martha had expected it to be. Relieved, she allowed herself to be ushered out the door and down the porch steps.

A cool breeze carried the scent of Tristan's aftershave. Pine needles and campfire smoke, crisp fall air and winter wind. Everything outdoorsy and good. All the things Marti loved most about God's creation.

"Thanks again for saving my life, Tristan. I know you said I saved myself, but we both know it's not true."

"Do we?" He took the keys from her hand, unlocked the door and carried the key chain with him as he rounded the car.

"Hey! I need those if I'm going to get to church."

"I know. I'll give them back to you in a second." He opened the passenger door, slid into the car and held the keys out to her, a grin easing the hard angles of his face.

Her heart leaped, her brain froze. He was in her car. In. Her. Car. And she had absolutely no idea what to do about it. She leaned in the open door, stared him in the eye, hoping she looked less flustered than she felt. "What are you doing?"

"Making sure you get to church in one piece."

"I've been driving to church on my own for years. I'm sure I can manage it today."

"Unless you run into Johnson."

"He won't try anything in the middle of broad daylight when anyone might see him." At least, she didn't think he would.

"Sunshine, you don't know much about men like Johnson. He's not going to just forget that you saw him Friday, that you heard his name, that you could sit in court and identify him. He and I both saw your name on the card inside your pack. There's no way he forgot it. He's going to come after you and he's not going to wait until it's dark, or you're alone, or until some time when it's convenient for you. He'll strike when he's good and ready. For all either of us know, he's ready now. Until he's caught, you need to be careful."

"I know I need to be careful. And I will, but that doesn't mean having a personal bodyguard."

"I think it does." He grabbed her hand, tugged her farther

into the car. "And since I took a bullet for you, I think I should have some say in these things."

"I can't believe you're using that against me after you said I saved my own life."

"Whatever works, Sunshine." He tugged hard, and she almost tumbled across the seat and into his lap.

"It's Marti, not Sunshine." She muttered the words as she pulled away from his grip and settled into the driver's seat.

"Right. Martha Darlene Gabler. Born September 18. Twenty-eight years old. Two and a half years of college. Working as a veterinary technician at Lakeview Veterinary Clinic. Recently engaged. Even more recently no longer engaged."

"I'm not even surprised you know all that about me."

"There's more."

"Of course there's more. Since I know myself pretty well, and you now seem to know everything about me, let's save some time and not rehash all the details of my boring life."

"Who said anything about boring?"

"Compared to yours—"

"Why would you? Compare your life to mine, I mean?" He watched her with those striking eyes, leaning toward her, his body language, his posture saying he was really listening. That he really wanted to hear what she had to say.

Which was, of course, part of the courting game and meant absolutely nothing.

Courting?

As if.

Men like Tristan Sinclair did not notice women like Marti, let alone court them.

"I'm not comparing. I'm just saying that my life is pretty mundane and yours…well, yours isn't."

"I've got news for you, Marti. Your life is anything but mundane right now. And, by the time this is all over, you're going to be wishing for boring." The words were a grim reminder that Gordon Johnson was free, and Marti's hands tightened into fists around the steering wheel.

"You really think Johnson is coming after me?"

"I don't think it. I know it. Johnson is a lot of things, but stupid isn't one of them. He knows you're bound to be the state's key witness against Buddy and him. He's going to make it his goal to keep you from testifying."

"That's not very comforting."

"Good. The less comfortable you are, the happier I'll be."

"Gee, thanks." She shoved the keys in the ignition, but he put a hand over hers before she could start the car.

"Johnson is a cold-blooded killer, Marti. If making you uncomfortable keeps you safe from him, that's exactly what I want to do."

"Look, Tristan, I know you're trying to help, but—"

"I'm not *trying* to do anything. I'm doing it." He squeezed her hand, the gesture easy and warm. "Now, let's go. We don't want to be late."

She should keep arguing, tell him to get out, remind him that she was a grown woman capable of taking care of herself, but something told her that Tristan Sinclair was not going to be dissuaded and that short of getting out and walking to church, Marti had no choice but to accept her unwanted passenger.

Or maybe not so unwanted.

The fact was, having Tristan around didn't seem like such a bad thing. As she pulled up her long driveway, she imagined a million eyes watching from the woods that lined the street, a million dangers lurking just out of sight. Silly, she knew, but as real as the air she was breathing. Anyone could be hiding in the thick fall foliage, ready to jump in front of the car, shoot out a tire, force her to a stop. And if that anyone happened to be Gordon Johnson, Marti figured that having Tristan in her car might not be such a bad idea after all.

SIX

Chocolate. Cinnamon. The warmth of family mixed with the cool, crisp fall breeze.

Tristan had smelled more exotic perfumes, but none had tugged at his awareness the way Martha's scent did. It hovered around her as he escorted her through the church parking lot and made him want to inhale, to hold the fragrance deep in his lungs, let it fill the part of him that had been emptied during the months he'd worked undercover.

A time of renewal.

He needed that as much as he needed to get the cast off his arm and get himself back into working shape.

"I'll be fine from here." Marti spoke quietly as they approached the church's open front door. It seemed she actually thought he was going to leave her there.

"I know, but I think I'll join you anyway."

"You might want to rethink that. I'm planning to volunteer in the toddler nursery." They might not need her there, but at least closed in the nursery, Martha knew she could avoid the questions her women's Sunday School class was bound to ask.

"And you think that will scare me away?"

"I've seen lesser men felled by the prospect."

Tristan laughed, the sound dry and a little harsh. It had been a while since he'd found anything to be truly amused about. Life as Sky Davis hadn't been something to laugh at. "Good thing I'm not lesser men."

She leaned back, giving him a slow appraising look that was more joke than flirtation. "Yes, it is."

He laughed again, hooking his good arm around her waist and tugging her the last few feet to the church door. "Thanks for the laugh, Sunshine."

"Thanks for playing bodyguard. Of course you know that as soon as church is over, I'm sending you on your way."

"I know you'll try."

"Martha!" The strident male voice greeted them as they stepped into the building. The speaker, a lean blonde with hard eyes and a weak jaw, hurried toward them, his gaze on Martha: "I've been trying to call you all weekend."

Marti stiffened as he approached, but her smile was pleasant. Unless Tristan missed his guess, this was the fiancé. The ex-fiancé.

"Yes. I know."

"And you didn't think it necessary to answer the phone, or to return the calls?"

"A lot of people were calling me, Brian. I couldn't get to everyone."

Brian. Yep, the ex-fiancé.

"If you organized your time better that wouldn't be a problem. What you should have done was make a list and—"

"Prioritize. Yes, Brian. I know. Fortunately, that's not something you need to concern yourself about anymore." Marti smiled again, her teeth gritted in an obvious effort to keep from saying something she'd regret.

Tristan had no such compunction. "I'm sure you did prioritize, Sunshine. There's no doubt in my mind you managed to contact the people who warranted it."

Brian frowned, seeming to notice Tristan for the first time since the conversation had begun. His dark gaze dropped to the arm Tristan had wrapped around Marti's waist, his frown deepening. "I don't think we've met."

"You're right. We haven't. I'm Tristan Sinclair." He offered his hand, not surprised that Brian put a little too much strength in the shake. He was a man who seemed determined to be the top dog. Unfortunately, he was probably closer to being the runt of the litter.

"Brian McMath. Martha's *good* friend."

"I wouldn't exactly call us friends, Brian."

"Of course we're friends. Just because we broke up doesn't mean we don't still care about each other. As a matter of fact, I've been thinking that we could—"

"Don't we need to get to the nursery?" Tristan cut off what threatened to be a long-winded attempt to win Martha back.

"Yes, we do. Nice seeing you, Brian." Martha moved away, and Tristan started to follow only to be pulled up short by Brian's hand on his shoulder.

"I think we need to talk."

"Do you?" Tristan eyed the other man, wondering what Martha had seen in him. Obviously he had an overblown sense of importance and a penchant for cutting people down.

"You may not know this, but Martha and I were engaged."

"I'd heard talk of it." While Tristan lay in a hospital bed recovering from surgery on his arm, his brother Grayson had spent the previous day gathering information. A Lakeview local who'd transplanted from their childhood home in Forest, Virginia, Grayson was a lawyer and good at getting the information he wanted.

"Good. Then you'll understand my concern. She's vulnerable right now. It's going to take her a while to get over our breakup."

"I heard Martha broke up with you. I doubt it'll take her long to recover from that."

Brian's face went scarlet and his eyes flashed. "No one broke up with anyone. It was a mutual decision."

"If that's the way you want to see it." Tristan didn't know why he felt the urge to needle the man. Sure, the guy was arrogant, but most of the time Tristan ignored people like him. Then again, most of the time, he didn't have to deal with arrogant jerks masquerading as caring Christians.

"Look, my point is that Martha needs time to recover from everything that's happened to her. A relationship at this point would only be a rebound reaction to her loss. It's probably best if you give her some space."

Space? Not likely. At least, not until Johnson was found. "I think I'll let her tell me that. If you'll excuse me, I promised to help her this morning." He strode away before McMath could respond, just catching sight of Martha's deep blue dress as she hurried into a room at the end of the hall.

Tristan followed, peering into the nursery and grimacing as he caught sight of his worst nightmare—fifteen kids the size of peanuts waddling around crying, giggling and babbling. Cute, but dangerous. He'd learned that the hard way on more than one occasion.

He stepped inside, closing the door firmly behind him. Three women eyed him with curiosity. The fourth studiously avoided glancing in his direction. Too bad. He wouldn't mind getting another look in Martha's gold-green eyes.

"Ladies." He tipped his head in greeting and used his good arm to lift a rambunctious little girl from the floor. The angelic-looking kid gave him an impish grin and popped him in the nose. "Hey, that hurt!"

"Better watch out for that one. She's got a reputation for making boys cry." An older lady with salt-and-pepper hair and amused blue eyes pulled the little girl from his arm. "I'm Anna Patrick."

"Tristan Sinclair."

"Nice to meet you, Tristan, but I don't think you're on the nursery roster for this morning."

"I'm with Martha."

"With Martha?" Anna and the other women glanced in Martha's direction.

Martha's face went three shades of red, but she managed a smile. "We're…friends. Tristan offered to lend a hand in here today."

"*A* hand is right." A thirty-something blond woman with bright brown eyes and a quick smile gestured to Tristan's sling. "You're going to have a hard time with only one hand. This is a busy bunch of kids."

"He looks like the kind of guy who can handle anything." A sharp-faced brunette eyed Tristan from a rocking chair across the room. He recognized the interest in her gaze, the sharp gleam of a huntress on the prowl. He'd met plenty of women like her, had even dated a few. But women like her weren't what he was looking for. Not anymore. Now, he thought he might like to find someone more solid, more down-to-earth.

More like…well, Martha.

There. It was out. A truth he'd been avoiding since he'd awakened after surgery on his arm. Martha had been the first one he'd thought of. The only one he'd really wanted to see. Sure, he'd made conversation with his parents, his brothers and sister, the doctors and nurses and coworkers who'd been a streaming distraction while he lay in the hospital bed, but it had been Martha he'd wondered about. Martha he'd pictured over and over again. Gold-green eyes, wild curls. Strength and determination, wrapped up in a very attractive package. Thinking about Martha, wondering how she'd fared after the raid, had provided Tristan with more of a distraction than any of his visitors. Much as he might tell himself he was here to catch Johnson, the truth was a little more complicated. Sure, he wanted to stop Johnson, but he also wanted to keep Martha safe.

And get to know her.

No matter how bad of an idea it might be.

And it *was* a bad idea. The life he led didn't lend itself to family. It was stressful and hard. Not just on the men and women who worked the job, but on their families, as well.

"Why don't you come have a seat in one of the rocking chairs." The brunette waved him over. "You can tell us how you and Martha met."

"Thanks, but I've had a few too many days of forced rest. I think I'll stand for a while."

"Did you break your arm?" The brunette didn't seem to be getting the hint that Tristan wasn't interested, and Martha seemed determined to ignore them both rather than join in the conversation.

"Yes." He didn't add that a bullet had shattered the bone and that rods and pins were currently keeping things in place.

"You're probably one of those extreme-sports junkies. Skydiving. Snowboarding. That kind of stuff."

"Actually, I prefer long hikes in the mountains." He crossed the room and knelt on the floor next to Martha who was building a block tower with one of the toddlers.

She met his gaze, acknowledging his comment with a smile. There were freckles on her nose and cheeks that he'd noticed the first time he'd seen her. Cute freckles to go with the curls that were escaping the sleek hairstyle she'd managed.

"What?" She brushed a hand down her cheek. "Is there something on my face?"

"Just freckles."

She wrinkled her nose. "Don't remind me. They were the bane of my elementary-school years. Jeremiah Bentley used to call me Paint Splatter. Eventually that was shortened to Splat."

"Jeremiah must have had a serious crush on you."

"Jeremiah was a pest. Until tenth grade. Then he was captain of the football team. At that point I decided it was better to have him call me Splat than to not have him call me at all."

He chuckled, pulling a little boy away from another child's toy. "Captain of the football team, huh? And you were what? Head cheerleader?"

"Cheerleader? Hardly. I was more likely to be hiking through the woods than dancing and flipping in front of a crowd." Martha didn't add what she was thinking—that she'd never been one of the popular crowd, and that growing up without a mother had made it difficult to figure out the kind of girlie things that were so valued in high school. Makeup, hair, clothes. She'd learned them all by trial and error. And, she had to admit, there'd been a lot more error than success.

"Martha, a cheerleader? You don't know how funny that is." Jenny Gardner brushed a thick wave of dark hair from her forehead and stood, moving across the room, her hips swaying in her perfectly fitting knee-length skirt. She looked good and she knew it. But then, Jenny had never had a bad hair day in her life. Or at least, not in the fifteen years Martha had known her.

"Funny? Why?"

Of course, Tristan had to ask, and, of course, Jenny was more than willing to answer. Martha had seen the way she'd been eyeing the man in their midst. Like a chocoholic at a candy buffet.

"Martha was a science geek. Always outside traipsing around in the forest, coming into school with twigs and leaves in her hair, mud from feet to knees. I don't think she'd have ever cleaned up enough to be in a cheerleader uniform."

"A science geek, huh?" Tristan met Marti's gaze, his eyes bright blue and assessing, scanning her face, touching on the freckles that she had always hated. Under his intense but clearly approving stare, they didn't seem quite so bad.

"Half the time the poor dear looked more like a guy than a girl with her baggy pants and hooded sweatshirts."

Martha's cheeks heated, but she refused to be pulled into Jenny's grade-school behavior. Sure, she'd been a geek, but that was years ago. Now she was an accomplished, confident adult. Really. She was. "That was a long time ago, Jenny."

"True, but you still do love to wander around in the woods. That is how you ended up involved in that…incident… Friday, isn't it?"

"Incident? Marti could have been killed! I'd call that a little more than an incident." Anna jumped into the conversation, and Martha let her take over. She was too tired to go a verbal round with Jenny.

Martha stood, brushing off her dress. Deep sapphire blue, it had been a spur-of-the-moment purchase. One she'd regretted immediately. Brian had liked it, of course. The slim-fitting sheath had an air of sophistication that made her seem almost elegant. Almost.

And that was the problem. No matter how hard she tried, she could never measure up to women like Jenny who oozed style from every pore. In her opinion, it was better not to try at all than to end up looking like a want-to-be-fashionista.

She sighed, gently tugged a toddler from the nursery door. Why she was even thinking about her lack of style, she didn't know. She'd accepted herself for who she was long ago and didn't bother making apologies for it. So she liked to hike and camp more than she liked to shop for clothes. Was that a crime?

"You and I have a lot in common." Tristan moved up beside her, a pigtailed little girl in his arm.

"Do we?"

"I was a science geek, too."

"You? No way." She laughed, sure he only said that because he thought Jenny's comments had bothered her. They hadn't. Much.

"I was president of the science club three years running."

"Not four?"

"I would have been, but Sheryl Greeson wanted the position and I decided she could have it."

"She was cute?"

"Beautiful. And smart. Of course, she only had eyes for the captain of the football team. I wound up going to the prom with a cheerleader who had a thing for geeks."

She doubted it was Tristan's "geekiness" that had appealed to his prom date. "Well, I can one-up you on that. I didn't go to the prom."

The words slipped out before she thought them through, and she winced. She'd made herself seem pathetic.

Before she could try to rectify the error, Jenny spoke up. "Marti was too busy working. She was always one of those goody-goody daddy-girls. Too busy helping out at her father's store to cut loose and have a little fun."

"Some kids have to work, Jenny. That's just the way it is."

Cries filled the room as one toddler after another decided

to take up a chorus of tears. Much as Marti hated to hear them cry, at least the sound kept Jenny from commenting further.

Or Marti from saying anything else that might give Tristan the idea that she'd been a pitifully awkward teen.

Not that it mattered what ideas he had. She'd dated enough to know that she didn't want to waste more of her time mooning over a man. She'd been engaged long enough to know that it wasn't worth the hassle. No, from this point forward, she was man free and happy about it.

Tristan caught her eye as she scooped up one of the criers and smiled the kind of smile meant to melt female hearts. Marti's heart didn't melt, though. Maybe it softened a little, but it definitely didn't melt.

Because she really *was* happy about not having a man in her life. And she really planned on staying that way.

SEVEN

Church service started peacefully enough. Aside from the fact that Marti was sitting next to the best-looking man in the building, the day seemed like any other Sunday. If she tried hard enough, and avoided looking at Tristan, she might even be able to forget that she'd almost been killed two days before, that a murderer was wandering free and that he might be coming to find her.

"Doll! I thought you were staying home today." The raspy sound of her father's voice made Marti smile, and she stood to greet him as he moved down the aisle toward her. Though he'd been to her house the previous day, his eyes were lit as if he and Marti hadn't seen each other in months.

That was her dad. Her biggest fan. Her only fan.

"I thought I was, too, but I changed my mind at the last minute." Marti leaned forward and kissed him on the cheek, the leathery warmth of his skin as familiar as sunrise. "Where's your better half?"

"Chatting with some friends out in the hall. She'll be glad to see that you're okay. She's been worrying something fierce. We both have."

"There was no need. I'm right as rain."

"Doesn't matter. I still worry. That's what fathers are

supposed to do." His gaze shifted to the region beyond Marti's shoulder, and she had a feeling she knew what he was looking at. *Who* he was looking at.

She turned and saw that Tristan had moved up behind her, his silvery eyes focused on her father.

"Dad, I want you to meet Tristan Sinclair. He's a…friend of mine. Tristan, this is my father, Jesse Gabler."

"Nice to meet you, Mr. Gabler." Tristan extended a hand, his arm brushing Martha's as he leaned past her, the warmth of his body seeping through her dress and making Martha's cheeks heat.

"Call me Jesse. Most everyone does. You're a friend of Marti's, huh?"

"That's right."

"Where'd you meet?"

"Dad, the service is about to start. We don't have time for the third degree." She cut the conversation off before it could take wing. Knowing her father, he'd push for as many details as Tristan was willing to give. Right now, she didn't want him to give any. As soon as Dad found out who Tristan was, there'd be an explosion of questions. Maybe even of temper. Her dad was a lot of things, but meek and mild-mannered wasn't one of them.

"Then we'll talk about it over lunch. You are planning to join us for lunch, Tristan?"

"I'm sure he's got other plans." Martha shot Tristan a look that she hoped would convey her feelings about lunch—she didn't want to have it with him.

Either he misinterpreted her look, or he didn't care. "Actually, I don't. I'd love to have lunch with your family."

"Glad to hear it. Sue is always excited about an extra mouth to feed. Speaking of which, here she comes."

Sure enough, Sue was barreling toward them, her lively

green eyes riveted on Tristan, her squarish frame nearly humming with energy. Where Jesse was reserved and slow to act, Sue was outgoing and quick to rush into things.

She was also quick to speak, and Martha didn't think that now was a good time to have a conversation.

Martha took a step back, bumping into Tristan, her cheeks heating again as his hand cupped her shoulder and stayed there. What was with her? She was a grown woman. Not a kid with a crush. "Sorry. The music is starting. I think we'd better sit down."

"No one else is."

True. As was usual, the congregation of Grace Christian Church was too busy catching up on the week's events to settle quickly. "They will be."

She nudged him in the stomach with her elbow, and this time he got the hint, moving back into the pew without further comment. And just in time. The air turned thick with the flowery scent of Sue's perfume as Martha's stepmother settled into the pew beside her. "Martha, dear, I'm so glad you're here. I've been up all night worrying. I was just so sure Jesse and I should have stayed over at your house last night."

As always, words poured from Sue like bees from a hive, thick and quick and charming in their artlessness.

"I know and I appreciated the offer."

"Did you sleep well? You do look a little tired."

"I'm fine."

"So, no nightmares? You know, my mother used to make me a glass of warm milk before bed. She insisted that it would chase away any and all bad dreams."

"Maybe I'll try that tonight."

"You should. You really should. Now—" Sue peered around Martha, giving Tristan a more thorough look "—who are you, young man? A friend of Martha's?"

"Tristan Sinclair, ma'am."

"It's good that you can be with our Martha during this terrible time. She did tell you what happened Friday, didn't she?"

"Actually—"

"Service is starting." Martha cut Tristan off.

Tristan leaned close, his lips brushing her ear as he whispered, "Chicken."

"I am not. I just don't think now is the time to tell my father you were the man who kidnapped me." She hissed her reply, sure she'd fallen into an alternate reality. One minute, she'd been engaged to a doctor, doing her best to fit the impossibly polished shoes the position demanded. The next, she'd been a kidnapping victim, fighting for her life. And now, well, now, she was sitting in church with her father, her stepmother and a man who'd caught the attention of every single woman in the congregation.

Obviously her life had taken a wrong turn somewhere in the past week. She needed to figure out where she'd gone wrong and get back on course. Quickly.

Tristan's hand covered hers, stopping the unconscious tapping she'd been doing. Warm and callused, his palm pressed against her knuckles, his fingers linking with hers, deeply tan against her paler skin. He squeezed gently and released his hold, but the warmth of his touch remained.

She glanced his way, but his focus was on the pulpit and Pastor Avery, who'd begun to make the morning announcements. She knew her attention should be there as well, but she had trouble concentrating as announcements gave way to a hymn and then to the sermon.

The pastor's words of faith during adversity washed over Martha and through her, but she felt disconnected from the message. As much as she tried to concentrate, she couldn't hold on to anything the pastor said for longer than the few seconds it took him to say it. It didn't help that Sue's perfume was strong enough to clog her lungs and steal her breath. Halfway through the sermon Martha's eyes started to water. Her nose itched, and the urge to cough nearly overwhelmed her.

When the music minister stood to lead the last hymn, Martha eased past Sue and her father and hurried out the sanctuary door. The air outside was fresh and clean, the loamy scent of dying leaves and moist earth a welcome relief. Martha took a deep breath, trying to clear her lungs and her head.

"Next time, let me know before you go running off." Tristan's words made her jump, and she whirled to face him.

"You nearly gave me heart failure. Warn a girl next time."

"That's better than what Johnson would have given you if he'd found you out here alone."

"There's no way he'd know to find me here." She tried to sound confident, but Tristan's warning was one she knew she should heed. Going outside alone when a crazy man wanted her dead probably wasn't the best idea she'd ever had.

Tristan touched her arm, his fingers warm through the silky material of her dress. "Listen, Sunshine, I can do my job better if you cooperate. No more going outside without me. Okay?"

"Okay."

"Good. Sounds like the service has ended. How about we go have that lunch your dad promised me?"

"I'm still not sure I want you having lunch with us. There's no telling what my father will do when he finds out—"

"That I kidnapped you?" He grinned, his eyes the bright blue of the autumn sky.

She couldn't stop her answering grin. "Exactly. Of course, I'll also have to tell him that you saved my life, so that should even things out."

"Martha!" Sue bustled toward them, weaving her way through the crowd exiting the church. "Is everything okay? I was worried when you left so suddenly, but since Tristan followed you out, I knew you'd be fine."

"You were right. I was. I just needed a breath of fresh air."

"After all you've been through, dear, I'm not surprised." Her gaze drifted from Martha's face to Tristan's hand, which was still resting on Martha's arm. "You know, if you two were planning a special date, we can skip lunch—"

"A date? Us? No way." Martha nearly snorted at the thought.

"Don't sound so amused by the idea, Sunshine. It could happen."

"Not in this lifetime."

"Never say never, Martha." Sue smiled, looking more than happy to be witness to the interplay between them. "But since it isn't happening today, I'm glad to have you both for some good old-fashioned southern-fried chicken and potato salad. *And* your dad started some of those yeast rolls you love so much, dear."

"It sounds wonderful. I can't wait to eat." But for the first time in as long as Martha could remember, the thought of food didn't appeal. It was amazing how almost getting killed could ruin a person's appetite.

"We'll see you at your dad's place in a few minutes then. You, too, Tristan. Bring your appetite. What with my boys all grown and gone, I've always got way too much food left over."

"I'm more than willing to do my part to rectify that situation, ma'am."

"Call me Sue. 'Ma'am' makes me feel old. Now, I'm going to find Jesse and get him moving. Otherwise, lunch won't be ready until supper time! You two get a move on, and I'll see you at the house."

"I guess we've got our orders." Tristan cupped Martha's

elbow, merging into a crowd of people moving toward their cars. He scanned the parking lot as he moved, looking for danger but not finding it.

"And I'm sure we'll get more before the day is through. Sue is a steel magnolia." Martha smiled up into his eyes, her lips curving.

And Tristan's mind jumped back forty-eight hours, remembering cool rain washing down his face as he leaned toward Martha, felt the softness of her lips, breathed in chocolate and cinnamon. It had been an action designed to fool Gordon Johnson. But it had pulled him in, become more. That was something Tristan couldn't quite understand.

He'd met a lot of women during his years working for the ATF. Many of them were from the darker side of life; some, like Martha, were innocents who had been drawn into circumstances beyond their control. None of them had affected him the way Martha did.

Maybe she sensed the direction of his thoughts, because she stiffened, her muscles tensing under his hand. "You know, you don't really have to come to lunch, Tristan. I'm sure you've got other plans, and I know I'll be safe inside Dad and Sue's place. As a matter of fact, I'll even promise to stay away from the windows."

"Thanks, but you are the only thing I have planned for this weekend. Actually, for the week." Maybe longer if that's what it took to bring Johnson in and ensure Martha's safety.

"You're not serious."

"Sunshine, I'm more than serious. Until Johnson is found, you and I are going to be joined at the hip."

"Eventually you'll have to go home and get back to work."

"I'm on medical leave. For now, keeping you safe is my work."

"Tristan—"

"How about we discuss it after lunch? I don't know about you, but I think better on a full stomach." He cut her off before she could argue more. It would be a waste of both their energy. He'd already made up his mind. Whether Martha liked it or not, he was sticking around. He'd told his boss that, had even asked for backup, but Daniel Sampson hadn't been convinced that Johnson would make a move against Martha.

Tristan was. The sole civilian witness to his crimes and Buddy's, Martha was the state's key witness. Johnson would definitely try to get rid of her. It was just a matter of time.

EIGHT

Martha knew that having lunch with Tristan, Sue and her dad wasn't a good idea. There were just too many things that could go wrong. Dad could lay into Tristan, accusing him of reckless endangerment when he found out the role Tristan had played in Friday's trouble. Worse, he could break out Martha's baby pictures and brag about what a cute kid she'd been. Sue could fill Tristan in on all the details of Martha's relationship with Brian, explaining in excruciating detail her opinions on why things had gone wrong. Tristan could…well…he could be Tristan. Handsome, confident. Admirable. And Dad could start getting ideas about marriage and grandkids.

Five minutes passed as fried chicken was piled onto plates, potato salad and dinner rolls made their rounds and Sue regaled her guests with stories of her volunteer work at the hospital. The flow of conversation took on an easy, comfortable feel, and Martha started to relax, to believe that the meal might pass without any of the things she'd been worried about.

She should have known better.

"So, Tristan, tell us, how did you and Marti meet?" Sue's bright tone belied the intense curiosity in her gaze. The poor woman just couldn't help it. She was a born gossip. Or maybe collector of information was a better name for it. She might spread the information she gathered, but never with malicious intent.

"We met in the mountains on Friday."

"What?" Jesse set his fork down on the table, and sent a hard look in Martha's direction.

"I was working the gun raid."

"He's the man I told you about. Sky Davis. Remember?"

"The criminal? The guy who kidnapped you? Sitting at my table?" Jesse stood, and Martha had a quick vision of her father lunging for Tristan.

"Actually, Mr. Gabler, I'm an ATF agent. I was working undercover when Martha and I met."

"You nearly got my daughter killed!"

"Dad, he saved my life. I told you that."

"Sit down, Jesse. Sit down right now and eat. I won't have you ruining my meal with your temper. Tristan, I can't tell you how glad I am that you were there the day Martha ran into her trouble." Sue took a sip of sweet tea, her bright eyes filled with excitement. Martha could almost imagine her cataloguing Tristan's words, filing them under "juicy tidbits."

"I'm glad I was there, too." Tristan met Martha's eyes, and she was sure she saw humor in his gaze.

"Martha said you were shot trying to protect her. Is that where you got your arm injury? From the bullet?"

"I'm afraid so."

"And now you're in town to make sure Martha's okay? That's just so romanti—"

"Sue, I'm sure Tristan didn't come here to answer a hundred questions." Martha tried to stop the flow of conversation, but like the tide, it just kept rolling in.

"Actually, Sue, one of our perpetrators escaped Friday."

"This just keeps getting better and better. First I meet the man who nearly got my daughter killed—"

"He saved my life, Dad," Martha repeated.

"And now I find out a criminal mastermind is on the loose."

"Not for long, Mr. Gabler. We'll have him in custody soon."

"Says the man who nearly got my—"

"Dad!"

Jesse scowled. "Sorry, doll, but it's the way I see it."

"I'd see it the same way if it were my daughter." Tristan's words seemed to mollify Jesse, and he settled back into his chair.

"You think this guy is coming to Lakeview? Coming after Martha?"

"It's a good possibility."

"Well, put her in one of those witness protection programs, then. A safe house. Someplace where the guy won't find her."

"I tried. My boss isn't convinced she's in danger."

"Give me his number. I'll call and make sure he is."

"You're welcome to try. I've already spent hours doing the same. Now I'm here, and I'll do everything in my power to make sure your daughter stays safe."

"Everything in your power. You want to explain what that means? Twenty-four-hour guard? Patrol cars in front of her place? What?"

Marti sighed. It was going to be a long afternoon. "I'm going to clean the kitchen."

She grabbed her plate and exited the room, relieved when Sue didn't follow her into the kitchen. Not that she'd expected her stepmother to. The conversation at the table was a lot more interesting than loading a dishwasher. Though, for her part, Martha could think of a lot of things she'd rather do than discuss scary possibilities and twenty-four-hour guards.

She grabbed a pan from the stove, scraped the contents into

Sue's compost bucket and did the same with several bowls. Ten minutes later, she'd managed to empty the dishwasher, fill it again and wipe down the counters, but the conversation in the dining room was still going strong. She could hear just enough of it to know that her name was being mentioned over and over again. If Martha were brave enough, she'd march back into the room and tell all three of them that she'd prefer a change in subject.

She wasn't, so she'd just wait things out and deal with her father, Sue and Tristan one at a time. Starting with Tristan. If his boss didn't think Martha was in danger, then there was no reason for Tristan to play bodyguard. She'd tell him that on the way back to her place.

Just the thought made her feel better than she had all day. Once she sent Tristan on his way, she could get back to her normal routine. Tomorrow she'd go to work, immerse herself in her job and forget Friday had ever happened. Eventually the nightmares would go away and she'd stop jumping at shadows.

She grabbed the compost bucket and opened the back door. Outside, cold sunlight shone off dry grass and colorful leaves. The air was sweet with autumn, the sky vividly blue. In years past, the Gablers' corner lot had been scraggly and neglected. Sue had changed that, surrounding the large yard with a five-foot fence that she'd painted white, planting vegetable and flower gardens, creating order out of disorder. Marti smiled a little as she carried the bucket toward the compost pile at the back edge of the yard. Sue and Jesse Gabler were an unlikely pair, but a good one, and she was glad her father had finally found someone he could trust with his heart.

"At least *he* won't be spending the rest of his days alone." She dumped the compost on top of the pile, and turned toward the house just as an engine roared to life. A dark blue pickup drove by, U-turned in a neighbor's driveway and started back, picking up speed as it went. Surprised, Martha turned to watch its approach. A kid, probably. No one else would drive that fast through the neighborhood.

The truck jumped the curb, heading right toward the fence, not slowing as it ran over the grass.

"Get out of the way!" Tristan's warning barely registered as Martha jumped back, tumbling in her haste, landing on the ground and rolling away as metal and wood collided. Fence planks snapped; shards of lumber rained down.

"Stay down!" Tristan shouted the order as Martha struggled to her knees, his arms wrapping around her waist as he pressed her back onto the ground, holding her still when she would have levered up.

They stayed that way, his chest against her back, his lips close to her ear as wood crunched, tires squealed and the sound of the engine faded away.

In the stillness that followed, Martha could hear nothing but her frantically pounding heart and the harsh rasp of her breath. Then other things registered—Tristan's more controlled breathing, Sue's cries of alarm, her father's heavy footfall as he crossed the yard.

"What's going on? What happened?" Her father's raspy voice seemed to break through the terror that held Martha immobile. She shifted, and Tristan moved with her, standing and pulling her to her feet.

"Are you okay?" He brushed hair from her eyes and framed her face with his hands, his palms warm against her icy skin.

"I think so." Though she wasn't sure her shaking legs would hold her much longer.

"Can someone please tell me what's going on?" Martha's

father raked a hand through his thinning hair, his gaze skimming over the broken fence before settling on Martha.

"A truck driver lost control and rammed the fence," she said.

"The driver did not lose control." Tristan's voice was harsh.

"What are you saying?" Sue nearly squeaked the question, but Tristan didn't respond.

His focus was on Martha, his eyes a deep, stormy blue. "What were you doing out here by yourself? I thought we agreed you'd stay inside."

"I was putting scraps in the compost pile. And this *is* inside. Or pretty close to it. The entire yard is fenced."

"Which is about as useful as a piece of paper for protecting a person from a bullet."

"No one shot at me. Someone drove into a fence. For all we know, it was an accident."

"It wasn't an accident." Tristan bit out each word, clearly enunciating, as if doing so would convince Martha.

But she didn't want to be convinced, because that would mean admitting Johnson had found her. "He couldn't have found Dad's house so quickly."

"He could. He did." Tristan's words were harsh, his grip tight as he hurried her back to the house.

"I'm going to call the police." Sue hurried inside, and Martha glanced at the broken fence, her heart still beating too fast. *Had* Johnson been at the wheel of the truck? Things had happened too fast for Martha to see. She couldn't say for sure that he hadn't been.

"Someone is going to pay for this." Her father pushed at splintered wood with his foot, but he sounded more worried than angry.

"Dad? Are you coming inside?"

"Yes, then I'm going out. I've got some business to attend to."

"What kind of business, Mr. Gabler?" Tristan nudged Martha inside the house. Her father followed them.

"I'm going to find that truck. I caught a good look at it. Dark blue Chevy. Two-door. It's got to have some scratches on the front bumper."

"I got a good look at it, too, and saw what direction it went in. If you stay here and wait for the police, I'll take Martha's car and go look."

"I think I'd rather go looking."

"Then who'll be here with Martha and Sue?"

"You should *both* stay here with us and wait for the police." The thought of either man chasing after Johnson made Martha's stomach churn.

"Babe, I *am* the police." Tristan snagged Martha's keys from the hall table where she'd dropped them when she'd arrived.

"The one-armed police."

"So?"

"So, I don't want you to get hurt again."

"I won't." He stepped out the front door, and short of grabbing the keys from his hands, there wasn't a lot Martha could do to stop him.

"Tristan, I really don't like this."

"Neither do I. Do me a favor and stay inside this time. I don't want anything to happen to you while I'm gone."

"You listen to him, doll. I come back and find out you're out looking for trouble and my heart might give out."

"I think you'd better stay and keep an eye on her, Mr. Gabler."

"Jesse. And I'm going. With you or on my own. Your choice." Tristan hesitated, then nodded. "Then we'll go together."

"Let's get going then. We'll take my car." Jesse kissed Martha on the cheek and hurried outside.

Tristan followed, tucking Martha's keys into his pocket as

he went. Obviously, he had every intention of making sure she didn't join the hunt. He hadn't bothered putting on his jacket, and the white straps of his sling were visible against his dark shirt. How much of a chance would he have against Johnson? Not enough. And having her seventy-year-old father along for the ride didn't increase his odds of success.

"Tristan?"

He paused with his hand on the car door. "Yeah?"

"Are you left-handed or right-handed?"

He laughed, shook his head. "I'm ambidextrous. Now go inside."

She did. Closed the door, turned the lock. "Lord, please keep them safe."

She whispered the prayer as she walked down the hall, wishing she could do more. Prayer was good, but sometimes life demanded action. Unfortunately, in this case action wasn't a possibility. She had to wait. Wait for the police. Wait for Tristan and her father to return. Wait to see how it all unfolded.

"Your father went off with him, didn't he?" Sue grabbed Martha's arm as she walked back into the kitchen.

"Yes."

"He's a brave man, your dad, but he's not as young as he used to be. And when he gets back I'm going to tell him exactly what I think of him going off after a killer." Her voice broke, and Martha put her hand on Sue's shoulder.

"It'll be okay. They'll be back before we know it."

"I hope so."

"I know so. Sit down. I'll make us some tea while we wait."

"That sounds lovely, dear."

Lovely. Definitely not a term Martha would use to describe anything about the day. She bit back a sigh, set the kettle on to boil and waited, her mind filling with images—the smashed fence and speeding truck, Tristan's arm dripping blood as men raced through the trees. Johnson's cold gaze.

He'd kill anyone who got in his way. Tristan. Martha's father. *Anyone.*

Much as Martha wanted him off the streets, she wanted Tristan and her father safe more. She couldn't help praying that if it really had been Johnson in the truck, they wouldn't find him.

NINE

Time ticked by slowly as Martha waited.

Really slowly.

The police came and went. Martha drank two cups of tea and ate three chocolate-chip cookies. Sue made five phone calls. And still Tristan and Jesse didn't return. Finally, Martha couldn't take it anymore. She grabbed another chocolate-chip cookie, pilfered her spare keys from the kitchen drawer where her father kept them and eased open the front door.

She probably shouldn't be doing this. She probably should stay in the house where it was safe and listen to another few hours of Sue going over all the details of what had happened with friends, family and acquaintances. She probably should, but she couldn't. The men had been gone for three hours. That was a long time to be out searching for a truck. Something must have happened. They could have been in an accident. The car may have broken down. Or worse, they might have found what they were looking for. Just the thought of her father getting close to Johnson made Martha shiver as she got in her car.

She glanced in the rearview mirror and started backing out of the driveway, but slammed on the brakes when a car pulled in behind her. Her father's car. Finally. Relief filled her as Tristan got out of the vehicle and stalked to her door, pulling it open and tugging her out before she even had a chance to turn off the engine.

"Didn't I tell you to stay inside?" He barked the question, his scowl storm-cloud dark.

"You've been gone three hours. *Three.*"

"I don't care if it was a hundred. You shouldn't have come out here."

"What was I supposed to do? Sit in the house and wait forever for you two to come back?"

"If that's what it took, yeah." He ran a hand over his hair, obviously trying to rein in his temper before he spoke again.

"Well, I couldn't. I was worried. I needed to know that you guys were okay."

"We're grown men, Sunshine. Perfectly capable of taking care of ourselves."

"And I'm a grown woman. Also capable of taking care of myself."

"You're also the one Johnson wants dead."

"I doubt he's got any fondness for you, either."

"If he thinks I'm in jail, I'm safe."

"If. That's not very likely."

He shook his head, a half smile chasing some of the anger from his face. "You need to stop worrying so much about me and start worrying about yourself. Where'd you get the keys to your car?"

"I had a spare set. Should have thought of that before I left." Jesse spoke as he moved up beside Tristan. "Of course, I didn't expect Martha to come traipsing outside like there was nothing to worry about. This Johnson guy, he doesn't play games, doll. He's a cold-blooded killer." Obviously, Jesse and Tristan had done a lot of talking during the past hours and were now in complete agreement on the situation.

"Don't worry, Dad. I know."

"Good. Now I'd better go inside and apologize to Sue. I doubt she's happy that I went off without telling her what I was doing." He pushed open the front door and disappeared inside, leaving Martha and Tristan standing beside Martha's car. Just the two of them. Again. It seemed they kept returning to that.

"I guess you didn't find him." Martha knew that wasn't good, but she was too relieved that her father and Tristan were okay to dwell on it.

"No, but not for lack of trying. We drove through the neighborhood, knocked on doors, talked to people. A few saw the truck. None noticed who was in the driver's seat."

"Thanks for trying."

"I'd thank you for staying where I left you, but since you didn't, I won't."

"I'm not good at sitting around waiting."

"Yeah. I'm getting that. You know, Sunshine, you're more trouble than I bargained for when I went into those mountains on Friday." Tristan looked down into her face, studying it, searching it. She wasn't sure what he was looking for, but she doubted he'd find it. She was who she was. There was nothing hidden or mysterious about her.

"At least you were bargaining on trouble. I was looking for a nice peaceful getaway."

"Nice and peaceful, huh?" His fingers curled around her elbow, and he urged her to get back in the car. "I thought you said your life was mundane. Seems like there'd be plenty of peace in that."

"The past week has been hectic."

"You mean because you broke up with that Brian guy."

Surprised, she met Tristan's eyes. "How'd you know we broke up this week?"

"People talk. Give them an opportunity and they'll tell you just about anything you want to know."

"I suppose there's a reason you're telling me this."

"It isn't going to be hard for Johnson to find out everything he wants to about your life and your habits. He saw your name and address in your backpack. A few questions to the right people and he'll be staking out every place you go."

"Every place I go? You're talking work, home, the movies, the local diner. He won't have any trouble at all finding me." Despite the seriousness of the situation, Martha laughed. Nerves did that to her. And she was nervous. Scared. Anxious.

She caught her breath, wiped at eyes that were streaming and met Tristan's gaze. *He* wasn't laughing. That much was for sure.

"Sorry about that. Sometimes I laugh when I'm scared."

"You don't have to apologize. You just have to take the danger seriously."

"Trust me, I do. I saw Johnson's eyes. There was nothing human there."

"You've hit the nail on the head, Martha. He's got no conscience. Nothing to keep him from doing things most of us wouldn't even imagine." He cupped her jaw, stared into her eyes, and she found herself sinking into his gaze.

"I know."

"So next time, do what I say, okay? It's the only way to make sure you stay safe. And I do want you safe." His eyes were almost hypnotic, his voice soothing, cajoling. Martha imagined most women would do exactly what he asked simply because he was the one asking.

She blinked and pulled away from his touch, starting the engine and driving toward home, determined not to fall for his charm. "You're good at getting what you want, Tristan Sinclair."

"Thanks. I've had a lot of practice."

"You date a lot?"

He laughed, the warmth of it rumbling out into the car and chasing away some of Martha's fear. "I actually practiced on my parents. I have three brothers and a sister. I learned young that getting what I wanted involved finesse rather than fit-throwing."

"So you were one of those spoiled golden boys? The kind who always got what he wanted because he was charming?"

"Hardly, but I sure gave it a run for the money. I used to keep a scorecard—how many times I convinced my parents to let me have my way as opposed to how many times my brothers or sister did."

"You did not!" She met his gaze, saw the laughter in his eyes.

"I did."

"So, did you get your way the most?"

"Not even close. My brother Grayson, he took the lead. Followed by my sister."

"I'm surprised your sister wasn't the clear winner what with her being the only girl."

"Don't be. My brother grew up to become a lawyer. He puts his persuasive skills to good use every day."

"Good career choice."

"We thought so."

"And you became an ATF agent so you could force people to do what you wanted."

"Actually, I became an ATF agent to change the world. Sometimes I think I just might be doing that." He spoke quietly, and Martha dared a look in his direction. He was staring out the window, scanning the trees that lined her long driveway. Looking for signs Johnson was there waiting for a chance to strike.

"Do you think he's out there?"

"No, but let's not take chances. Park close to the porch."

Martha did as he said, opening the door and running inside, Tristan right beside her. "Thanks for the escort, Tristan."

"No problem. And, Sunshine?" He grabbed her hand and pulled her to a stop.

"Yes?" She turned, her breath hitching as she met his gaze.

"For the record, I've gotten a whole lot better at getting what I want."

Her cheeks flamed and her heart did a strange little dance. She told herself it had more to do with fatigue than with the man who was staring down into her eyes. "I'll keep that in mind."

"You do that." He released her hand, pushed the front door open again. "I'll see you in the morning."

"You're going home?" *You're leaving me here alone when Johnson might be lurking in the woods just out of sight?* That's what she was really thinking. Thank goodness she had enough self-control not to say it.

"Actually, I'll be outside in my car. That's where I'm camping out until Johnson is caught."

"Your car?"

"I can't stay in here. Your father wouldn't approve."

"You're actually planning to sleep out there in your car?"

"I've slept in a lot worse places over the years."

"But—"

"You're a half mile from your nearest neighbor, Martha. You don't have a security system. Your phone lines are so easy to cut a child could do it. If Johnson decides to come calling, I don't want you to be alone."

That was great, because she didn't want to be alone either. "Look, if you're really set on staying…" Her voice trailed off as she realized what she was about to say. What she was about to offer.

"What?"

Don't do it. Do *not* offer him the apartment over the garage. That will just make things too convenient and cozy. "There's an efficiency over the garage. The previous owner used to rent it to college students. It's empty. If you want, you can use it."

Of course, she did exactly what she shouldn't and offered him the place.

"How far is it from the house?"

"Not far. It's just out back." She led him out back to the square two-story building. A 1960s addition to Martha's turn-of-the-century home, the single-car garage stood less than a hundred feet from the back of the house. It had been a while since Martha had been inside the efficiency, and it took her a few seconds to find the key. When she did, the door squeaked open, the sound shivering along her nerves. Night hadn't fallen yet, but it would soon. She wanted to be locked in the house with every light on before then.

"Here it is. Like I said, it's not much. I don't even have furniture in here." She stepped into the large room, and Tristan followed, his arm brushing against her shoulder as he moved past her.

"I don't need furniture tonight. Maybe tomorrow I can get my brother to bring me a few things."

"Your brother is in the area?"

"Grayson lives about ten minutes away in a huge house filled with stuff he's not using. I don't think he'll miss a futon and a couple of pots and pans." As he spoke, Tristan strode across the room and pulled a dusty curtain back from one of the windows. "There's a good view of your back door from here." He seemed to be speaking more to himself than to Martha, but she crossed the room anyway, looking out onto her backyard.

"Do you want to stay here?"

"It beats sleeping in my car."

"I'll bring you a sleeping bag and a radio so it won't be too quiet out here."

"Quiet is good, so don't bother with the radio. I wouldn't mind a couple of aspirin, though."

"Is your arm bothering you?"

"Yeah."

"A lot?"

"Like a hot iron is being poked through it."

"Ouch."

"Exactly. Come on, let's go." He took her hand, his fingers warm and rough against her softer skin. Funny, Martha had never thought of herself as feminine and petite, but Tristan made her feel small and delicate.

Delicate? She almost snorted at the thought. She'd never been delicate, and she never would be.

"Stay here. It will only take me a minute to get the stuff." She tried to tug away from his hand, but he held firm.

"I think we'll do this my way instead."

"What way is that?"

"We'll go together."

"That's really—"

"Not necessary?"

"Okay. Maybe it is, but it does seem a little bit like overkill, don't you think?"

"What's overkill? Me walking back to the house with you?"

"It's a ten-second walk."

"A lot can happen in ten seconds, Martha. You saw that truck today. It jumped the curb and hit your father's fence in the blink of an eye."

He was right. A lot *could* happen in ten seconds. An engagement could be broken. A mother could abandon her child. A life could be snuffed out.

And a woman who'd said she'd never have anything to do with men again could find herself falling into deep blue eyes. Again.

TEN

Knowing Tristan was sleeping a hundred feet from the house should have made it easier for Martha to rest, but at 2:00 a.m. she was still awake. Every time she closed her eyes, she saw Gordon Johnson. And looking into his face wasn't restful. She supposed she could try counting sheep, but that would require closing her eyes and she'd already decided against that. Turning on the television and watching reruns of sitcoms was another option, but she was afraid the sound would mask other things. Like someone cutting out a pane of glass, turning the lock of the window and opening it. Easing inside. Creeping down the hall.

Martha shivered and shoved aside the blanket she'd been burrowing under. She was not going to spend the hours until sunrise imagining the worst. If she couldn't sleep, she might as well do something constructive. Like find chocolate. One good thing about living alone—there was no one she needed to explain an early-morning chocolate raid to. No one to witness a bad case of bed head, two-sizes-too-big flannel pajamas or floppy pink bunny slippers. No one to keep awake with her restless fear.

No one to share her worries.

To tell her everything was going to be all right.

She shook her head, knowing that wasn't the truth. She wasn't alone. God was with her. She could share her worries with Him, and she could trust that He'd take care of her. She knew that, but sometimes it was hard to feel the emptiness of the house and know that it might always be the same. Just Martha. No husband. No kids. No busy days wrapped around a life of domesticity.

Maybe it was silly to want those things, but she did.

More than that, though, she wanted what God intended for her life. After her experience with Brian, she was pretty certain that marriage wasn't what He had planned. That was okay, because as much as she might want a forever-after kind of relationship, she wasn't sure how good she'd be at it. Her parents hadn't been a great example of how to make things work. And her mother certainly hadn't shown Martha how to mother a child, unless walking out on your kid when she was five was the way to do it.

She flicked on the light in the kitchen, scrounged through the cupboards in search of her chocolate fix. Her supply was sparse. Two chocolate bars. A bag of M&Ms with peanuts. A few Hershey's Kisses. She unwrapped one, popping it in her mouth as she set the teakettle to boil. So what if she couldn't sleep? It wasn't the end of the world. Plenty of people suffered from insomnia. As a matter of fact, she was sure if she went online she'd find a support group for people who couldn't sleep. And one for people who'd dumped their fiancés. Maybe even one for women who were being stalked by killers.

A soft tap sounded at the back door, and Martha nearly dropped her teacup. For a moment she wasn't sure what to do. Ask who was there? Turn off the light and hide? Call the police?

The knock sounded again, this time more insistent. She grabbed a steak knife and crept toward the door, her heart racing. "Who's there?"

"Tristan."

She nearly sagged with relief, her heart slowing, and then jumping again as she opened the door and met Tristan's vivid blue gaze. "You're supposed to be in the garage apartment."

"And you're supposed to be asleep. Apparently neither of us are doing what we're supposed to."

"Is everything okay?"

"That's what I was going to ask you. When I saw your light go on, I thought I'd better come over and make sure you were okay."

"I'm fine. Just having trouble sleeping."

"So you're wandering around the house with a steak knife in your hand and pink bunny slippers on your feet?" A hint of a smile eased the harsh angles of his face, his gaze dropping from her eyes to her feet and back again.

"They seemed like a good idea at the time."

"When was that?"

"When I didn't think there'd be anyone in the house at two in the morning to see them." She placed the knife on the counter as his warm laughter filled the room, resisting the urge to smooth her hair. There was no way she could fix the mess she knew it to be, so there was no sense drawing more attention to it.

"I guess we've both been surprised, then, because I wasn't expecting to see a light on in your house at two in the morning." He smiled again, grabbing a Hershey's Kiss from the counter, his presence reminding Martha of all the things she needed to forget—namely, how nice it was to have someone to count on. Someone stronger, tougher, more able to fight if fighting needed doing. Not that Brian had been much of a fighter. He'd been more likely to argue and complain.

She really needed to stop comparing Tristan and Brian,

because doing so only painted Tristan in a more positive light than she wanted to see him. As she watched, he grabbed another chocolate, denting her limited supply.

See? Selfish. She'd known if she'd look hard enough she could find something negative about him. "Those chocolates are mine, you know."

"Didn't anyone ever teach you to share?" He popped the candy into his mouth and took a seat at the table.

"Didn't anyone ever teach you to ask?"

He laughed, grabbing another candy and eating it before Martha could snatch it from his hand. "I've got four siblings, remember? We all learned to grab what we could while we could. Besides, I'm hungry. I need to stock the fridge in the apartment tomorrow."

"If you're hungry, I've got sandwich makings in the fridge. Just leave my chocolate alone."

"Chocolate is a girl's best friend?"

"Absolutely."

"But it's not such good company at two in the morning, is it?" He looked up into her eyes, compassion shining from his gaze.

But she didn't want his compassion, because if she accepted it, she'd also be accepting his presence in her life. A presence that was becoming much too familiar much too quickly.

She turned away, pouring water over a tea bag, trying to put distance between them. "Want some tea?"

"No, thanks. I wouldn't mind a soda, though, if you have any."

"Soda at two in the morning?"

"Why not?"

"Good question." She grabbed a can of soda from the fridge, set it down in front of Tristan. Efficient. Businesslike. That was the way to handle this situation. "You asked me why I was up, but you didn't mention why you were."

"Probably the same reason you are—I'm worried."

"Because of what happened today?"

"Because of what happened Friday, what happened today. What might happen tomorrow and the next day." He ran his hand down his jaw and shook his head. "I know worry doesn't do any good, but my mind is running around in circles trying to figure out what Johnson's next move is going to be."

"I don't think anyone can do that."

"Maybe not, but I'm going to try." He stood, pacing across the room. He wasn't wearing his sling, and he held his injured arm close to his waist, shrugging his shoulder as if trying to relieve tension.

He might be saying he couldn't sleep because he was worried, but Martha wondered if the reason had a more physical cause. "Is your arm bothering you?"

"It's not too bad."

"That's not an answer."

"It hurts. Happy now?" He scowled, taking a sip of soda and eyeing Martha with an intensity that made her squirm.

"No, I'm not happy. I haven't been happy since Friday." Actually, she hadn't been happy in a couple of months. As much as she'd told herself she was, as much as she'd tried to pretend excitement over wedding preparation and engagement parties, there'd been a hollow ache in her chest that no amount of self-talk or pretend enthusiasm could fill.

She turned away from Tristan's gaze, grabbing a bottle of Tylenol from the cupboard and opening it. "Here, take these."

"Thanks." His fingers brushed her palm as he took the medicine, and she was sure they lingered for a moment longer than necessary. No. She had to have been wrong about that. There was nothing between Tristan and herself but the need to find Johnson and put him in jail.

She needed to keep that in mind.

In the distance, a car engine chugged along, growing closer. So close that Martha stiffened, cocking her head and straining to hear more. "I think someone is coming up my driveway."

"Sounds like it."

"You don't seem concerned."

"I called the local sheriff a few hours ago. He agreed to send patrol cars out as often as possible. It's probably one of them. Stay here while I make sure that's who it is."

"But—"

"Are you going fight me on everything, Sunshine?"

"No, I just—"

"Good. I'll be back in a minute." He pulled a gun that Martha hadn't even realized he was carrying, and her heart froze in her chest.

"What are you doing?"

"Taking care of things. Stay here." He strode away, not giving Martha a chance to ask more questions, or demand answers. The soft hum of the engine came closer, and Martha knew the car would be passing the house, U-turning at the dead end, moving by again. Or would it? Maybe it would stop. Maybe the sharp, quick blast of bullets would fill the silence.

Legs trembling, she grabbed the phone, ready to call 911 at the first hint of trouble.

Then she followed Tristan. He might not like it, but he couldn't change it, and there was no way in the world she was going to cower in the kitchen while he faced danger alone. It wasn't what her father had raised her to do.

Be tough. Be strong. The world's gonna knock you down. You got to learn to bounce back up again.

She could almost hear him saying the words, could picture his gnarled hands pulling back branches as he led her on long hikes through the woods, teaching her about survival and about life. Too bad he hadn't told her what to do if a murderer came knocking on the door.

She moved silently, easing down the hallway, making sure that she avoided loose floorboards. The last thing she wanted to do was distract Tristan.

The darkness of the living room was as oppressive as her fear, sucking away her confidence and making her want to slink back into the kitchen and do exactly what she'd decided she wouldn't. Hide from the trouble. Let Tristan take control.

At the window, a shade darker than the room, Tristan stood pressed against the wall with his broken arm holding back the curtain, his good arm holding the gun. Focused. Intent. "I told you to stay in the kitchen."

She hadn't made a sound, but somehow Tristan had known she was there. "I thought you might need some help."

"Looking outside?" He didn't turn toward her as he spoke, just continued to stare out the window.

"Calling the police."

"Thanks, but if Johnson had been out there, I'd have acted first and called the police later."

"But he wasn't."

"No, he wasn't. But that doesn't mean he won't be next time."

"I know."

"Do you, Sunshine? Because you sure don't act like it." He dropped the curtain and tucked the gun out of sight again.

"How should I act? Like a damsel in distress who needs a prince to run to her rescue?"

"Like a woman who'd rather be alive than dead." Even in the darkness, she could see his eyes flashing with irritation.

"Of course I'd rather be alive."

"Then maybe next time I tell you to stay put, you'll do it."

"And maybe next time you'll actually give me something to do besides sitting around twiddling my thumbs."

He stared at her for a moment, his grim expression slowly easing into a smile. "You're stubborn as a mule, Sunshine, you know that?"

"How could I not? Brian told me that just about every day for eighteen months." The words slipped out and Martha blushed. Fortunately, it was too dark for Tristan to see.

"Brian is a real winner."

"That and a few other things." Like arrogant. Self-centered. Thoughtless.

"But you almost married the guy anyway?"

Ouch! That hurt, but she refused to let Tristan know it. "I like to call our engagement nine months of temporary insanity."

"Nine *months* of temporary insanity?"

"Yes. Fortunately, I'm over it now."

He chuckled, but Martha wasn't amused. She really had been out of her mind to consider marriage to a guy like Brian. Not that he was a bad guy. It was more that he wasn't the kind of guy who'd ever put another person's needs above his own. He was the kind who'd demand more and more and never be satisfied. The kind of person her mother had been.

She'd learned her lesson. There'd be no more trying to be someone she wasn't. The thought of the months she'd wasted doing just that made her feel more tired than she had all weekend. "It's late. We should both probably try to get some sleep."

"You're right, but there's something I want to ask you first." Tristan grabbed her wrist before she could take a step away, his thumb pressed against the pulse point there. Could he feel the way her heart jumped? The sudden speeding of her pulse?

She sure could, and she didn't like it.

If men could still be heroes, if chivalry were still practiced and dragons were still in need of slaying, Tristan would be in the front line of every battle; the knight that every maiden wanted as her champion. A guardian of truth, a protector of the innocent. A man who made women swoon and other men jealous. Someone who could be very, very dangerous to Martha's heart if she let him. She had no intention of letting him. "What's that?"

"How is it that a woman like you ended up engaged to a guy like Brian?"

"The same way any woman ends up engaged to any man. Brian asked. I said yes."

"That's not what I mean, and you know it."

"Maybe, but your question is presumptuous and *you* know it. We barely know each other. Neither of us should be asking questions about the other's relationships."

"You're wrong there, Sunshine. We know each other a lot more than 'barely.' After what happened Friday, I'd say we know each other well."

"Why? Because you kissed me?". Twice. Not that she'd been counting.

"Actually, I hadn't thought about that, but thanks for the reminder."

Martha's cheeks heated. "We didn't even know each other's names Friday, let alone anything else."

"I knew your name. I saw it in your backpack, remember? I also saw that you were strong, independent. A fighter. That you pack more chocolate than protein bars when you hike through the woods, and that when the going gets tough you just keep going. Oh yeah—" he leaned in close, inhaling deeply "—I learned that you smell like a memory and a promise—chocolate and cinnamon all rolled into one."

There went her heart again, skipping and jumping and

acting more foolish than it ever had when she'd been around Brian. "Tristan—"

"You deserve a lot better than a man like Brian, Sunshine. I'm glad you realized it." His lips touched hers, the contact so brief Martha could almost believe she'd imagined it. Almost.

"Lock the door." He left before Martha could respond, moving through the room and disappearing out the back door as quickly as he'd arrived, the house falling silent behind him.

Alone again.

Just the way she should want it.

She turned off the kitchen light and retreated to her bedroom. It had been a long day. Tomorrow would be longer. The best thing she could do was forget her worries and concentrate on getting the rest she needed. But as she settled into her bed, she couldn't deny the truth. As much as she might want to convince herself otherwise, alone really wasn't what she wanted to be.

ELEVEN

Tristan's cell phone rang at a little past seven in the morning. He'd been awake for an hour by then, and he scowled as he saw his older brother Grayson's phone number on the display. "It's seven o'clock."

"And?"

"And you said you'd give me a six o'clock wake-up call."

"You want a wake-up call, go stay in a hotel."

"I can't stay in a hotel and do my job at the same time."

"What job? You're on medical leave."

"That doesn't mean I'm not working."

"You shouldn't be." The oldest of the five Sinclair siblings, Grayson had definite ideas about what his brothers and sister should and should not do.

"That's my choice to make."

"That doesn't mean I have to like it."

"You're trying to tell me you're worried?" Tristan nearly snorted at the thought. Grayson was a lot of things, but he wasn't a worrier. As a matter of fact, he'd talked Tristan into more than his fair share of trouble when they were teens.

"*Mom* is worried. I'm just disgusted that you'd go to such great lengths to get out of painting our parents' house."

"It's that time already?" They'd been helping their father

paint the hundred-year-old farmhouse they'd grown up in since they were old enough to lift a brush. Every three years they'd congregate at the old house and enjoy each other's company while they made sure the house looked bright and cheerful as per their mother's orders.

"First weekend in November, just like always."

"I thought we painted two years ago."

"Three. We painted the year I met…" He didn't finish, but Tristan knew exactly what he was going to say—the year he'd met Maria. A woman Tristan had never liked, and who, he had to admit, he was glad his brother had decided not to marry.

"That's right. I forgot. I may be able to make it if things here wrap up quickly."

"Somehow I don't think that's going to happen."

"Why not? Gordon Johnson isn't known for patience."

"He's also not known for stupidity." Grayson had good reason to know. A state prosecutor, he knew plenty about Gordon Johnson and his boss.

"True. One way or another, though, I'll be around when he decides to make his move." Tristan crossed the room and looked out the window. Martha's house shone brilliant white in the first rays of morning light, the windows reflecting the navy blue sky and the gold and red leaves of the trees that surrounded the property. A wide creek, filled from the fall rain, meandered through autumn-brown grass. At another time, Tristan would have appreciated the quiet beauty and peaceful tranquillity of the place. Now all he could do was see the potential for danger.

"Just be careful, bro. Johnson and Buddy have avoided prosecution for a long time. There's no way either plans to have that change now."

"Understood."

"Good. Do you need anything for your late-night stakeouts?"

"A futon. A chair. Some groceries."

"Seems like a lot to fit in one car."

"Martha's got an apartment over her garage. She offered it to me."

"And you accepted?"

"Yeah. Is there a problem with that?"

"No. I've just never known you to take the easy path in anything."

"What's easy about sleeping on the floor?"

"Good point. Listen, I've got an early meeting, so I've got to run. Give me the address and I'll drop off the stuff you need later in the day."

Tristan rattled off the house number and street address, then hung up and stepped outside. His arm throbbed and his body ached, but talking to his brother had lightened his mood. A mood that had been storm-cloud dark since he'd learned that Johnson had eluded capture. He'd wanted the man behind bars in a big way. Buddy might be the boss, but it was Johnson who carried out the orders. In Tristan's mind, that made him just as dangerous. Maybe more so.

Dry grass crunched under his feet as Tristan rounded the corner of the house and surveyed the front yard. Somewhere overhead a hawk called, the sound haunting in the still morning air. This was what life should be about—the beauty of God's creation. The harmony of nature. The peace that came from enjoying the bountiful gifts of the Creator.

Should be, but wasn't.

Much as he might appreciate the scenery, Tristan knew how fleeting peace was. Evil tainted every picturesque landscape. He'd seen it over and over again, and wouldn't be lulled into complacency by the sweet serenity the morning offered. That, he knew, was a surefire way to get killed.

A soft sound broke the stillness, and Tristan tensed, scanning the yard. Everything looked as it should, the rustle of leaves in the breeze the only movement. Maybe he'd imagined the sound.

Maybe.

And maybe something ugly was hidden behind nature's splendor. He pulled his gun, the cool metal a comforting weight in his hand. There it was again. The snap of a twig, the crunch of grass. Something big, but not Johnson. No way would the gunrunner announce his presence that way.

Tristan slid the weapon back into its holster, watching and waiting as the sounds drew closer. A figure stepped out from the thick stand of trees. Short. Athletic build. Wearing a bright green jacket, jeans and hiking boots. Martha. Tristan scowled as she moved into the clearing, completely oblivious to his presence, her focus on something she held in a towel.

Sunlight danced off golden hair and highlighted the smoothness of her skin. Cheeks pink from the cold, her hair a mop of wild curls, she looked pretty and compelling and much too vulnerable for Tristan's comfort.

"What are you doing out here?" His tone was harsher than he intended, his frustration and his worry coming out in a near bark that made Martha jump and spin toward him. "Tristan! You nearly scared the life out of me."

"Better to have it scared out of you than choked out of you. I thought we agreed that you weren't going to wander around alone."

"I'm not alone." She glanced over her shoulder, looked confused for a moment, then shrugged. "At least, I wasn't. I guess Eldridge got sidetracked somewhere."

"Eldridge?" She'd been out taking a walk in the early-morning hours with a *man*. Tristan knew he should be happy that she hadn't been outside alone, but the thought of her taking a romantic stroll with another man didn't do much to his happy meter.

"My mailman."

Could it get any better? If Tristan's arm hadn't been throbbing so badly he might have laughed. "You and your mailman are in the habit of taking early-morning strolls together?"

"Eldridge lives across the creek on the other side of the woods. *He's* in the habit of taking early-morning strolls and sometimes he stops here for coffee before he goes home."

"I see." And he didn't like it. Martha and her mail carrier out on romantic hikes through the woods. No, he didn't like it at all.

"Today he found this little guy." She moved toward Tristan, peeling back the towel and revealing a scrawny cat whose torn ear and feral hiss made Tristan want to pull the creature from Martha's hands and let it go back to whatever back alley it had come from.

"He looks mean."

"He's hurt. Eldridge asked me to help catch him so I could take him to the vet clinic." She dropped the towel back over the cat's head, bright red scratches visible on her knuckles and wrist.

Tristan grabbed her hand, tugging her close so that he could examine the wounds, his fingers wrapped around warm, soft flesh. "These need to be cleaned and bandaged."

"I'll do it after I get a carrier for Fluffy."

"Fluffy? That cat is scrawnier than a scarecrow without stuffing."

"He won't be once we get him cleaned up and treated, and put some groceries in him."

Tristan wasn't convinced, but decided not to say as much. Standing out front of Martha's house chatting about the reha-

bilitation of a scruffy cat wasn't high on his list of safe things
to do. "Where's the carrier?"

"I've got three or four out in the garage." She started around
the side of the house, but Tristan pulled her up short.

"I'll take the cat and get the carrier. You go inside and take
care of those scratches."

"I can't let you lug around a squirming cat when you've
got a broken arm."

"Who said anything about letting me? Give me the cat and
go inside. It's not safe out here."

"Everything okay?" A man stepped out from the trees, his
dark gaze dropping from Tristan's face to his hand, which was
still on Martha's arm.

"Fine." Martha smiled warmly, her eyes glowing vivid
green and burnished gold. "Come over and meet Tristan. He's
the agent I was telling you about."

"The one that's staying out in the apartment?" The man
moved toward them. Tall. A few years older than Tristan, he
had a guarded smile and was carrying a handful of bright
orange and yellow leaves.

"That's right. Tristan, this is Eldridge Grady. Mail carrier
and distant neighbor. Eldridge, Tristan Sinclair. ATF agent."

"Good to meet you." Tristan offered his hand and was surprised by Eldridge's firm shake. Not aggressive or territo-
rial as some men got when a woman they were interested in
was close by.

"You, too. Thanks for taking care of Marti. My wife and I
have been worried about her since she had that run-in with
trouble Friday."

Wife? Apparently Tristan had completely misread the situation. Suddenly, his bottom-of-the-barrel mood lifted. "I'm
worried about her, too. That's why I was asking her to go

inside. Until we capture the man I'm looking for, Martha needs to stay behind closed doors as much as possible."

Eldridge turned his attention to Martha, scowling darkly. "Why didn't you tell me you were still in danger? I never would have asked for your help if I'd known."

"I—"

"Give me the cat and get yourself inside. Mary won't ever forgive me if something happens to you because I couldn't catch a mangy cat myself." Eldridge grabbed the cat from her hands.

"Fluffy isn't—"

"Go inside." Tristan turned to Eldridge as Marti finally disappeared inside the house. "Is she always this stubborn?"

"More, but she's got a good heart. Not enough people in this world are like that. You stickin' around for a while?"

"Until I'm a hundred percent convinced Martha will be safe if I leave."

"Good to know. Come on. Let's get this feral beast into a carrier before he decides to start fighting for freedom again and I drop precious cargo."

"I wouldn't call that cat precious."

"I'm talking about the leaves, man. If I go home without them I'll be in the doghouse for a month." Eldridge nodded toward the leaves he still clutched in his hand.

"Your wife collects leaves?" Tristan took the bundle of gold and red foliage from Eldridge.

"Nah. She's got a fall project planned for her kindergarten class and she needs leaves for it. And don't ask me what the project is. She was telling me during the Cowboys game yesterday and the information got lost somewhere in translation."

"You're a Cowboys fan?"

"Is there any other football team?"

"I could name a few." Tristan tried the garage door, frowning when it opened easily. "Martha needs to be more careful."

"I've been telling her that since she moved out here, but she hasn't listened. I can't tell you the number of times I've delivered mail and found her windows opened."

"Tell me you're kidding."

"Would I kid you about something like that?"

"I guess not. Which carrier do you want? Red? Green? Purple?"

"One is as good as another. I don't think the cat is gonna care. Just grab something, quick. My wife is probably staring at the clock thinking she's going to be late to work if I don't hurry it up."

"Then Fluffy gets purple." Tristan set the leaves down, opened the carrier door. "Here you go."

Eldridge maneuvered the cat in and closed the door. "There. He's ready for transport."

"Thanks for your help."

"I did it for Martha. She's a great lady. I'd hate to see her get hurt."

"I feel the same."

"Yeah?" Eldridge reached down and grabbed the leaves before spearing Tristan with a hard, dark look. "Well, there are all different ways of hurting people, aren't there? Keep that in mind, will you, Sinclair? Martha's had a rough life. She doesn't need any more trouble in it." He strode away before Tristan could respond.

It was for the best.

There wasn't a whole lot Tristan could say. He knew a warning when he heard it, and telling Eldridge he had no intention of hurting Martha wouldn't make any difference. People said things like that all the time. It was their actions that mattered. And Tristan had every intention of taking action. Martha would be safe. He'd make sure of that.

The cat yowled, pulling Tristan from his thoughts.

Time to go. The clock was ticking. Johnson was getting closer. And knowing Martha, she was already heading back outside.

TWELVE

The veterinary clinic's waiting room was crowded when Martha arrived at work. She wasn't surprised. People in Lakeview were curious. Some would say downright nosy. Dogs barked, cats hissed and yowled, people stared and whispered as she moved through the room.

Martha was almost glad Tristan was with her. At least people were getting their money's worth. They'd leave with a story to tell—Martha Gabler escorted by a hunky ATF agent.

She was *almost* glad, but not quite. Because eventually, Lord willing, the nightmare she was living would be over. Tristan would go back to his life. She'd return to hers. Martha could almost hear the conversations that would take place when that happened. All of them would begin with "poor Martha," end with "poor Martha" and have "poor Martha" sprinkled liberally in between.

And she didn't want to be "poor" Martha. Pitied Martha. Martha who'd grown up without a mother. Martha who'd had to help at her father's shop instead of hanging out with other kids during high school. She frowned, pushing open the door that separated the waiting area from the offices and exam rooms beyond. She'd thought she'd gotten over that years ago. Apparently too little sleep and too much fear were affecting her more than she'd thought they would.

"Martha, thank goodness you're here. The phones are ringing off the hook. The exam rooms are full. And to top it all off, Jessa McBride brought in her three dogs for a walk-in. I tried to tell her we were too busy, but she made such a fuss that I put her in room nine just to keep her from bothering our other clients. You'd think that woman was royalty the way she demands…" Lauren Parker's voice trailed off as she caught sight of Tristan and the cat carrier he held.

"Oh, sorry, I didn't realize you'd brought a patient back with you."

"I didn't. This is…" Who should she say Tristan was? A friend? A bodyguard? The man who'd saved her life? "Tristan Sinclair. He's helping me bring in a wounded cat. If you take care of Fluffy, I'll take care of Jessa." Martha took the carrier from Tristan and handed it over the counter before Lauren could ask questions she didn't want to answer.

"Fine by me. I'd rather deal with a feral cat than that woman." Lauren was still eyeing Tristan with blatant interest.

And why wouldn't she be? He was probably the best-looking man to set foot in the clinic since the doors opened three years ago.

Martha knew she shouldn't be bothered by Lauren's interest. After all, she had no claim on Tristan. Somehow, though, she was.

"Is Tori in yet?" Her question succeeded in drawing Lauren's attention away from Tristan.

"Her baby was fussy, so she's running a few minutes late. I told her we could handle things until she got here, but I didn't know things were going to be so hectic."

"How about Dr. Gerald?"

"He's not due in until ten. By that time, we'll have half the population of Lakeview complaining about our service."

"The good news is, our closest competitor is thirty miles away. Even if our clients are unhappy, they've got nowhere else to go." Martha attempted a smile as she hurried past the receptionist's desk and into a corridor lined with doors, doing her best to act as if this was any other day at work.

Of course it wasn't.

Tristan was right behind her, his presence impossible to ignore. Not just because Martha could hear his quiet footfall, but because she could feel him there.

Warmth. Strength. Confidence. They were as tangible and real as the first rays of sunlight after a storm. And just as welcome, even though she knew she shouldn't feel that way.

If she was smart, she'd turn around and tell him to go. Apparently, though, her brain cells weren't functioning today, because she couldn't muster the gumption to do it. Instead, she let him follow as she knocked on the door to room nine, braced herself and stepped inside. Three ratlike dogs rushed toward her, growling and barking in a high-pitched frenzy. Martha stood her ground. She'd dealt with Jessa's spoiled pooches enough to know they were all bark.

"Sheba, Sherry, Shelby! Cease!" Jessa walked toward Martha. No. She didn't walk. She glided, her head high, her dark skirt and pink blouse flawlessly tailored. Perfectly arched brows highlighted eyes that were blue today and might be green, purple or violet on her next visit. Collagen lips, Botox-smooth forehead, skin that was just a little too tight across her cheekbones and at the corner of her eyes, Jessa might have been forty or seventy.

Martha pegged her for mid-sixties and a lesson in what not to do as she grew older. Some things were meant to be—lines and wrinkles were two of them. "Jessa, how are you today?"

"It's not my health that's an issue."

"Lauren said this was an emergency visit. What's going on with the girls?"

"I'm surprised you need to ask. Can't you hear the problem?" Her gaze skittered from Martha to Tristan, her eyes widening. "Oh my. I didn't realize you had someone with you, Martha. Are you a new vet tech? Or perhaps a veterinarian? I didn't realize Tori was hiring someone else."

"Actually, ma'am, I'm neither of those. I'm here with Martha." Tristan's voice rumbled out and even the dogs seemed affected by it. They stilled, their beady little eyes riveted to the man in their midst.

Was no female immune to his charms?

Jessa obviously wasn't. She stepped closer, batting her fake eyelashes. "You're with Martha? As in—the two of you are together? What a surprise so soon after her engagement ended. And what a shock that was. We'd all hoped she'd finally found the man of her dreams."

"Brian wasn't nearly good enough for her, so I can't see how her breaking up with him would have surprised anyone."

Martha's cheeks heated, and she knew if she looked, she'd see amusement in Tristan's eyes. She chose not to look. "What he means is—"

"Exactly what I said."

"Oh my." Jessa's gaze jumped from Tristan to Martha and back again, and it was obvious she was already spinning the tale she'd tell her bridge club friends. "Well, then. I guess since things are so busy here today, I'll take my leave. You can set up an appointment for tomorrow, Martha, can't you? First thing in the morning, if you will. The girls are on their best behavior right after breakfast."

"Of course."

"I'll see you then, my dear." Jessa gathered her dogs' leashes, glided across the room to grab her purse, then returned to Martha's side, her long-nailed age-spot-free hand gripping Martha's bicep. "Do try to hold on to this one, Martha. You're not getting any younger, and soon the only catches you'll make will be old men or fathers of little hoodlums."

"Jessa!"

But Jessa was already heading down the corridor, her dogs barking and growling beside her.

"She's quite a lady." Tristan had moved closer, so close his breath ruffled Martha's hair as he spoke. If she turned, she'd be nose to nose with him. Or, rather, forehead to chin. Which was really close to lips to lips. Which was way too close for comfort.

"Yes. She is." And Tristan was quite a guy. A fact that Martha decided not to comment on.

She stepped away, moving down the corridor to the next door and pulling a file from the pocket there. Taylor Murphy and his guinea pig, Mop. "I'm going to check on the next patient. You can make yourself comfortable in the waiting area."

"I don't think so."

"So you're planning on following me around all day?"

"I am."

"I think that's unnecessary."

"I don't, so let's just play it my way and see how things go."

"Fine, but don't blame me if you're bored out of your mind inside of an hour."

"Sunshine, I could never be bored hanging out with you." He smiled, that easy, warm grin that made his eyes glow and his face soften, and Martha's traitorous heart did a little happy dance.

Who was she kidding?

It was a happy jig. A big one. The kind that was accompanied by bells and whistles and shooting stars. The kind it had done when Tristan had kissed her.

Three times.

Which was three times too many. She did not need a man in her life. The sooner her heart realized that, the happier she'd be. With that in mind, she did what any clear-thinking, romance-avoiding, smitten-with-a-guy-who'd-last-as-long-as-a-warm-day-in-the-Arctic woman would do. She ran, pushing open the door of the exam room and turning all her attention to Taylor and his pet.

Eight hours later, Martha had managed to answer several dozen questions regarding her health and well-being, field way too many questions about the illegal-weapons raid she'd been part of, assure dozens of well-meaning people that she was just fine and almost get used to Tristan's presence.

Almost.

She'd just filed the last chart and grabbed her jacket from a hook in the back room when her cell phone rang. She glanced at the number. "It's my dad. I'll just pick up the call. Then we can head out."

"Take your time. I'm in no hurry." Tristan leaned a shoulder against the wall and managed to look sincere, though Martha was sure he'd been ready to leave an hour after they'd arrived. Not that he'd complained. No, that would have made him too human.

And much less attractive.

She turned away from his steady gaze and answered the phone. "Hey, Dad. What's up?"

"Sue and I are going to be in your neighborhood tonight. We thought it might be nice to have dinner together."

"Dad, I'm a little tired."

"Too tired to spend time with your old man?"

"You're not old."

"Maybe not, but I'm pushing it. So, what do you say? Sue suggested we pick up Chinese food."

"Really, Dad, I've barely slept in three days, and I'm not sure I have the energy for company."

"Funny you should say that, I heard that you had plenty of energy for company last night."

"What?" Obviously, fatigue was playing tricks on her mind, because she was sure she must have misunderstood her father's words.

"Mary Grady saw Sue at the grocery store. She said you had a friend over last night. A male friend."

"Not a friend, Dad. Tristan."

"Thanks a lot." Tristan whispered the words so close to her ear, Martha felt the warmth of his breath.

She ignored him. At least, she tried to. "And I didn't have him over. I let him stay in the garage apartment. It was either that or leave him to sleep in his car."

"I'm glad to hear it, doll. I don't mind saying I'm worried about you. Having Tristan around makes me feel better."

"You don't need to worry Dad."

"Of course I do. I'm your father. It's my job."

"You're my father, and you taught me how to take care of myself."

"You keep bringing that up."

"Because it's true, Dad." Martha sighed, knowing that dinner with her father and Sue was inevitable. No way could she refuse. "Tell Sue Chinese food sounds great."

"You're sure?"

"Sure."

"Great. We'll see you in an hour."

"Right. Great." She mumbled the words as she tossed the phone into her purse.

HOW TO VALIDATE YOUR
EDITOR'S FREE GIFTS!
"THANK YOU"

1. Peel off the FREE GIFTS SEAL from front cover. Place it in the space provided at right. This automatically entitles you to receive two free books and two exciting surprise gifts.

2. Send back this card and you'll get 2 Love Inspired® Suspense books. These books are worth over $10, but are yours absolutely FREE!

3. There's no catch. You're under no obligation to buy anything. We charge nothing—ZERO—for your first shipment. And you don't have to make any minimum number of purchases—not even one!

4. We call this line Love Inspired Suspense because each month you'll receive books that are filled with riveting inspirational suspense. These tales of intrigue and romance feature Christian characters facing challenges to their faith and to their lives! You'll like the convenience of getting them delivered to your home well before they are in stores. And you'll love our discount prices, too!

5. We hope that after receiving your free books you'll want to remain a subscriber. But the choice is yours—to continue or cancel, anytime at all! So why not take us up on our invitation, with no risk of any kind. You'll be glad you did!

6. And remember. . . just for validating your Editor's Free Gifts Offer, we'll send you 2 books and 2 gifts, *ABSOLUTELY FREE!*

YOURS FREE!

We'll send you two fabulous surprise gifts (worth about $10) absolutely FREE, simply for accepting our no-risk offer!

The Editor's "Thank You" Free Gifts Include:

- Two inspirational suspense books
- Two exciting surprise gifts

YES!

PLACE
FREE GIFTS
SEAL
HERE

I have placed my Editor's "thank you" Free Gifts seal in the space provided above. Please send me the 2 FREE books and 2 FREE gifts for which I qualify. I understand that I am under no obligation to purchase anything further, as explained on the opposite page.

323 IDL ERWY   123 IDL ESWN

FIRST NAME   LAST NAME

ADDRESS

APT.#   CITY

STATE/PROV.   ZIP/POSTAL CODE

Thank You!

Order online at:
www.LoveInspiredSuspense.com

Steeple
Hill®

© 2008 STEEPLE HILL BOOKS

(LISUS-EC-08)

"I take it we're having dinner with your dad and Sue."

"*We're* not having dinner with anyone. I'm having dinner. You're going to do whatever it is you feel like doing after I'm safe inside my house." She knew she sounded waspish, and tried to curb her irritable mood, brushing back curls that had escaped their clip and meeting Tristan's eyes. "Sorry. That didn't come out the way I meant it."

"No need to apologize." He took her hand, his fingers linking with hers. "It's been a long day, but it's over. Now we can go home, have some Chinese food with your folks, enjoy a few hours of normalcy."

"Nothing about the last few days has been normal."

"No? It's been a while since I've lived anything close to what most people would consider a normal life, but I'd say spending time with people who care about you is about as normal as it gets." His fingers tightened around hers as he escorted her outside, and Martha couldn't help wondering what it was like to live undercover, how it was possible to be one person at the same time you were another.

Who was the real Tristan Sinclair?

What would it be like to discover the things that made him that person?

She pulled her thoughts away from dangerous territory. She did not want to know anything more about Tristan than she already did. Too much knowledge would only lead to eventual disappointment. Or worse. Expectations. And in that direction lay the path to heartache. Of that Martha was very, very sure.

She tugged her hand away from his, and climbed into her car. Being vulnerable stunk, and that's exactly how she felt. Vulnerable because her dream of marriage and family was gone. Vulnerable because she was about to be relegated to the position of old maid and she wasn't even thirty.

Vulnerable because Gordon Johnson wanted her dead.

Vulnerable because Tristan made her want to do exactly what she'd been raised not to do—rely on someone else.

Vulnerable.

Yeah, it stunk.

What stunk even more was that until Johnson was caught, she'd just have to keep on feeling that way. And maybe that was the point. Maybe God wanted her to realize she really couldn't do everything on her own. Maybe He wanted her to rely less on herself and more on Him. There was a lesson to be learned through the trials she was undergoing. She was sure of that. Eventually she'd figure out what it was.

If she lived long enough.

That unhappy thought followed her all the way back to her peaceful cottage in the woods.

THIRTEEN

Dinner was more comfortable than Martha expected. Sure, her father shot looks in Tristan's direction every few minutes, but Sue kept up a steady patter of conversation, and Tristan seemed happy enough to join in.

All in all, things went a lot better than Martha thought they would. By the time Sue served coffee and homemade sugar cookies, Martha was relaxed enough to enjoy her stepmother's less than subtle questioning of Tristan. It was nice to have her ATF agent bodyguard on the spot for a change. Not that Tristan seemed to mind. He answered every question, telling stories about his family, his childhood, his faith, his job.

The fact that he didn't get frustrated or annoyed with Sue would have raised him to the top of Martha's acceptable-husband-material list if she'd had one. Which she didn't.

Maybe that had been her problem all along.

Maybe if she had a list of acceptable characteristics, she wouldn't have spent so much time with Brian, whose brisk, sometimes irritated attitude toward Martha's family should have been the first clue as to where their relationship was headed.

Nowhere.

"Well, doll, this has been fun, but I've got to get Sue home. She turns into a pumpkin if we're out past ten."

"Me? You're the one who can't keep your eyes open after a good meal." Sue patted her husband's arm, her round face as comfortable and kind as an old friend. After all his years of being alone, Jesse seemed to be settling into married life with ease. Martha smiled as the two bantered back and forth, her gaze drifting to Tristan.

He met her eyes, his expression guarded, his gaze intense and searching. As if he could see something in her that others couldn't. As if he might know more than she wanted him to.

She stood, turning away from his probing gaze. "All right. Enough bickering about which one of you is more decrepit. You're both perfect. This really was a great evening. Thanks for coming over."

"You're right. It was fun, doll." Her father pulled her into a bear hug and kissed her cheek. "Thank you for letting us come."

"Letting you? You know you're always welcome here, Dad."

"I know I'm an old busybody who can't stand not knowing what's going on in his daughter's life. That's what I know. And I know you're a good daughter for putting up with me."

"I'm not putting up with anything. I love having you and Sue over. Whether I issue an invitation or not."

"Just as long as we don't wear out our welcome. Sue, you want to grab your purse and jacket and we'll get out of Marti's hair?" He strode down the hall and pulled the door open, draping an arm around Martha's shoulder and pulling her in for one last hug.

"Get away from the door. You're backlit." Tristan's sharp words were cut off as something slammed into Martha's shoulder. She spun sideways, blood spraying her face, her father shouting, shoving her hard, then falling beside her. Sue screamed. Tristan shouted again.

Glass shattered. Pain roared through Martha, but she barely

felt it over the wild pounding of fear. Johnson had come for her, just as Tristan had said he would, and the world as she knew it was over. The thoughts were quick staccato beats in her mind, the lights, the sounds, the smells all searing into her brain.

"Dad." She tried to sit up, but Tristan shoved her back down, covering her body with his own. A gun in his hand pointed out the open door. Firing. Once. Twice. Then there was silence, so deep, so black it stole Martha's breath.

"Don't move." Tristan's lips pressed against her ear as he levered forward and pushed the door shut. The soft click seemed to echo in Martha's head, spiraling in circles of color that made her stomach heave. She pushed up onto her elbows, and saw her father lying in a pool of blood, his chest covered in deep red as his life poured out.

"Dad!"

"I said, don't move." Tristan barked the command as he pressed his jacket against Jesse's chest. "Sue, call 911. Tell the dispatcher we need a Life Flight."

Life Flight. The words registered, but Martha couldn't allow herself to think about what they meant. She *wouldn't* allow herself to think about them, but they were there anyway, staining the wood floor, darkening the grain. Blood. Life. Oozing from her father.

She struggled to her knees, ignoring Tristan's next sharp command, to lean over her father, seeing his hazel eyes deep in a face so pale Martha thought he might already be gone.

"Don't worry, doll, I'll be fine." He wheezed the words out, and Martha's heart clenched.

"Of course you will. Just be quiet for now. Save your energy."

"For what? I don't think I'm gonna be doing much of anything for a while." He grinned, but his smile seemed to fade as his colorless face shrank in on itself, his eyes closing.

"Dad?"

"Lie down, Sunshine, before you fall down." Tristan growled the words, barking for towels in the same breath. Blood seeping over his hand, bubbling up from the dark, ugly wound in her father's chest.

Light faded. Sound diminished. Then returned. Louder. Brighter. Hands pressed Martha down. Concerned faces peered into hers. People shouted. Sirens blared. Mayhem and order all at the same time. Somewhere close by, a woman sobbed, the broken sound carrying over the cacophony of noise. Martha levered up, caught sight of Sue standing alone in the crowd, her face pale and streaked with tears.

"Sue—"

"You need to lie still, ma'am." Firm hands pressed Martha back down, and she looked up into concerned brown eyes.

"Is my father going to be okay?"

"They're airlifting him out."

Which wasn't an answer. Martha's brain was working enough for her to know that. "But is he going to be okay?"

"They'll do everything they can for him." The paramedic pressed another bandage to Martha's shoulder, holding it in place as he asked question after question that didn't matter until she finally shoved his hand away, and stood on shaky legs.

"Ma'am, you need to—"

"Find out what's going on with my father." Because he was the only real family she had. The one person who knew her and accepted her for who she was. The person who'd taught her what it meant to persist, to work hard, to have faith. To believe. In God. In people. In herself. And she wasn't going let them put him on a helicopter and fly him away before she said goodbye.

"Martha, it is Martha, right? You're going to do your father more harm than good if you get in the way of the medics who are treating him." The paramedic said something to the young woman next to him, and she nodded, moving toward Martha, speaking in the calm, soothing tones usually reserved for overwrought children. None of her words registered. None of what she said mattered. What mattered was seeing her father again. Just in case.

In case it was the last time. In case she never saw him alive again.

The ugly thought wouldn't leave, and Martha turned, her mind fuzzy as she tried to see past the people crowded around her father.

"Life Flight is two minutes out. Let's roll." A flurry of activity followed the shouted words, Sue's loud wail joining the frenzy of noise and activity.

Now Martha could see the stretcher being wheeled away. The small figure on it was the man who'd sung her lullabies in a rusty voice, who'd walked her to school on the first day of kindergarten, who'd dried her tears when she'd cried. Who'd been there when her mother had not. Steady. Sure. Unchanging through all the years of trouble they'd faced together.

"Can I just say goodbye?" The words barely escaped her dry throat, and she knew that no one heard them. That her father would be wheeled away, his life in the hands of doctors and nurses. And God.

Please, just let him be okay, Lord.

"Sunshine?" Tristan was suddenly in front of her, his eyes filled with worry, his harsh features softened with compassion. "You've got thirty seconds with your dad." He grabbed her hand, leading her through the crowd that parted as easily as it had closed ranks against her.

Her father lay pale and unmoving on the stretcher, his eyes

closed, his breathing shallow. If she could have spoken, Martha would have told him everything would be okay, but she couldn't speak past the tears in her throat. She just leaned forward, pressed a kiss to his forehead. "I love you, Daddy."

His eyes flickered open, his lips twitched into a smile. "Love you, too. Don't miss me too much, doll. You hear?"

Then they were rushing him away, toward the main road and the helicopter's thunderous approach.

"We need to take you to Lakeview Memorial, Martha. Let me help you onto the stretcher and we'll get going." The female paramedic put a hand on her arm, urging her toward another stretcher.

"Where are they taking my father?"

"Lynchburg General. It's farther away, but it's got a Level I trauma center."

"Then that's where I'm going, too." She shrugged away from the woman's hold. No way did she plan on going anywhere but where her father was.

"You're going to the hospital that's closest, Sunshine. When the doctor releases you, I'll take you to your dad."

"It might be too late by then." Martha's voice broke, and Tristan pulled her into his arms, feeling warm blood soaking through his shirt. She was still bleeding; not like her father, but enough for concern.

He stepped toward the stretcher, maneuvering her backward, wishing he had two good arms and not just one. "It won't be too late. Your dad is a tough guy. If anyone can pull through this he can."

"I need to be with him, Tristan. He's the only family I've got."

"Not now. Now he needs to be with the surgeons who are going to treat him."

"I can't just…let him go."

"No one is asking you to. We're just asking you to make sure that you're ready to help him when he needs it."

"Would you feel the same if it was your father they'd just taken away?" She looked up into his eyes, and he saw shock and a hollowness that he'd seen in the eyes of every victim he'd ever met. It made him cold with rage and with remorse. He should have warned Martha and her dad before they went to the front door. Should have been there in front of them, making sure Johnson didn't have his chance to steal one of their lives. He tamped down the emotions. He had to get Martha to the hospital. Then he'd go after Johnson and make sure he paid for what he'd done.

"I'd feel the way you do, babe. Scared and worried, but hopefully I'd have friends who'd make sure I got the treatment I needed anyway."

"This shouldn't have happened. How did it happen?"

"I don't know." He'd known Johnson would act, but he hadn't suspected the gunrunner would do so when there was so much room for error. With Tristan in the house. With witnesses around. With plenty of ways he could be seen or caught.

He should have known.

"But I do know this, I'm going to find Gordon Johnson, and I'm going to make sure he pays."

"It won't matter if my father dies."

"He won't." But even as he said it, Tristan knew that the chances of Jesse Gabler surviving were slim. The bullet had pierced his lung. Tristan had heard it in every gasping breath Martha's father had taken.

"Maybe I do need to go to the hospital." Martha swayed, and Tristan pulled her close, supporting her weight with one arm as paramedics rushed forward, lifting her, settling her onto the stretcher. Blood streamed from her shoulder, pooling beneath her and dripping onto the ground. Not as bad as her father, but bad enough.

It should not have happened.

He shouldn't have let it happen.

He clenched his jaw, shoving aside his anger. At himself. At Gordon Johnson. At his boss for not putting Martha in a safe house days ago.

"You're going to be okay, Sunshine." He brushed hair off her forehead, and was relieved when she opened her eyes.

She glanced over at her stepmother who was being given oxygen. "Will you take Sue to Lynchburg General and stay with her until we know what's happening with Dad?"

The desire to stay with Martha was so overpowering, Tristan almost said no. But the desperation in her eyes kept him silent. There were police everywhere, easing through grass and brush, searching for evidence that would lead to Johnson. Martha would be safe enough without him, but leaving her bleeding and scared was one of the hardest things he'd ever done.

"Whatever you need, Sunshine."

"That's what I need."

"Then I'll go. If you promise to stay at Lakeview Memorial until I can come get you."

"I promise."

"I'm going to hold you up to that." He trailed his knuckles across her cheekbone. Her skin was icy, but she forced a smile.

"Call me when you know something."

"I will." He let his hand drop, reluctantly moving away from Martha as they took her to the ambulance. When the doors to the ambulance closed, he turned to Sue, easing down onto the step beside her, covering her hand with his.

"Are you okay?"

"I don't know."

"Martha wants me to bring you to Lynchburg General. Are you up to it?"

"Yes. Thank you, Tristan."

He stood, offering his hand and gently pulling her to her feet. He'd do what he'd told Martha he would. He just prayed that when he called her he'd have good news rather than bad. He had to believe that's what he'd have. The world was full of ugliness, but sometimes there was a glimmer of beauty that couldn't be denied. A miracle that refused to be ignored. This was going to be one of those times. It had to be.

Lord, this time, let it be. Place Your hand upon Jesse Gabler so that he can return safely home to his wife. To Martha.

Tristan silently prayed as he escorted Sue to his car and drove her toward the hospital.

FOURTEEN

Martha prayed on her way to the hospital. She prayed as she was X-rayed and examined and as the deep gouge across the fleshy part of her shoulder was cleaned and stitched. She prayed while she was being questioned by the police and when she was left alone in a dimly lit hospital room, a television playing endless reruns.

And then she prayed some more while she waited, and waited and waited.

Please, God, let my father be okay. Please, God, let him live. Please let Tristan call me soon.

Please.

She pulled back the curtain and stared outside, smiling grimly when she realized she'd been put in a room that looked onto the roof of another part of the building. Four stories up. It would be all but impossible for Johnson to take a shot at her through the window. Obviously the police thought they were keeping her safe. If only they'd been as concerned about that *before* her father had been shot, then maybe he would have stayed safe.

Seconds ticked into minutes. Then into an hour. Then two. No one entered the room. The phone didn't ring. And like a prisoner waiting for release, Martha did nothing but pace and wonder if she'd ever get out. Her shoulder was numb, but her head ached with an insistent throbbing that made her stomach twist. Fear was a horrible beast, robbing the brain of the ability to think and the body of the ability to act. Martha knew she should do something, but couldn't decide what. Instead of calling Lynchburg General, or dialing Sue's cell phone, or calling friends who might come to keep her company, she paced the room. Scared of what a phone call might reveal, afraid that having friends close might put them in danger.

"I know you're with me, Lord, but I have never felt so alone in my life." She whispered the words as she settled onto the edge of the bed, her muscles so tense and sore that she felt closer to a hundred years old than to thirty.

A soft knock sounded on the door, and Martha braced herself for bad news as a police officer peered into the room. Older, maybe in his early sixties, his eyes were deep brown in nutmeg skin and so filled with compassion, Martha's throat tightened with tears she knew she couldn't allow herself to shed. Once she started crying, there was no way she'd be able to stop.

"Ms. Gabler? Dr. Brian McMath is asking to see you. He says he's a friend of yours. Do you know him?"

"Yes."

"Are you up to a visitor? Or would you rather I send him away?"

Under normal circumstances, Brian was the last person she would want to see, but these circumstances weren't normal and she wasn't sure what to do about his visit. Half of her wanted to send him away. The other half, the half that was terrified and lonely and unsure, wanted company no matter who that company might be.

"I…have you heard anything about my father?"

He shook his head. "I'm sorry. I haven't. I'll let you know if I do."

"Thank you."

"Should I send Dr. McMath away?"

There it was again. The same question that she hadn't known how to answer and still didn't. When had she forgotten how to make simple decisions? Probably at the same time she'd watched her father's blood seep out onto the floor. She shuddered. "No. That's okay. He can come in."

"All right. I'll be outside your room for the rest of the night, so if you need anything, just let me know."

"I will." But all she needed was to know that her father was okay and to hear that Johnson was behind bars, and no matter how hard she prayed, she just wasn't sure she would be hearing either any time soon.

The officer stepped back from the door, spoke quietly to someone else and then Brian walked into the room, his lab coat over a pristine shirt and muted tie, his hair perfectly combed and parted. Typical Brian. No matter how late the hour or busy the day, he always looked perfect.

"How are you feeling, Martha?" He spoke quietly, his words softer than she'd expected.

"I'm okay."

"I talked to your attending physician. You should be able to leave in the morning."

"Good."

"I also put in a call to Lynchburg General. Your father is in surgery. It may be hours before he's out."

Surprised, Martha met his gaze. "Thank you for checking on him for me."

"It's the least I could do under the circumstances." He cleared his throat, took a seat on the bed next to her. "Listen,

I'm really sorry this happened to you and your dad. I know we had our differences while we were dating, but I only ever wanted the best for you. Sometimes my way of expressing that leaves something to be desired."

An apology? From Brian? Like everything else that had happened, it seemed unreal. Part of a strange dream that Martha wanted to wake from but couldn't. "It's okay."

"It isn't, really." He sighed and stood. "Look, I just wanted to tell you I'm here if you need anything. And that I'll try to keep you updated on your father. I'm praying things go okay with the surgery, but I want you to know that it's going to be touch-and-go. Your father is older. He's in grave condition. You should prepare yourself."

Now he sounded more like the Brian she knew. Stating the facts with blunt disregard to her feelings. Much as she knew she needed to hear the truth, she wouldn't have minded having it couched in some pretty words of comfort. "How does a person prepare for something like this?"

He blinked, shook his head. "If I knew that, I'd be able to make things easier for a lot of people. Call my cell if you need anything."

He walked away, closing the door with a soft click and leaving Martha in silent darkness, his words hanging in the air.

Grave condition.

Touch-and-go.

She'd known it before Brian had said the words, but hearing them made it so much more real. More final. As if her father's death were a done deal. Over already while she sat twiddling her thumbs waiting for news. A hot tear escaped and slid down her cheek. She ignored it, holding herself still, holding her emotions in, trying to pretend the world wasn't falling apart while the pieces of it tumbled soundlessly around her.

"Lord, I really need to know that You're here. That everything will be okay. That I'm not as alone as I feel." She spoke the prayer out loud, her voice raspy and dry. Until now, she'd thought her faith capable of withstanding whatever the world might throw at it, but suddenly she wasn't quite as certain. It would be nice to have a sign, some tangible proof that God was intervening in ways she couldn't see.

She flopped onto her back, staring up at the ceiling and wishing she was as sure of things as she'd been a week ago. There was something to be said for going through life naively believing things would always stay the same. Of course, she'd known they'd change. She'd just never imagined they'd change like this. That during the course of a few days, everything she held dear could be threatened.

On the far wall a clock ticked the endless minutes as Martha waited for news. Twice, she placed a call to Lynchburg General. Twice, she was told her father was still in surgery. That was better than the alternative. Much better. But Martha could take little comfort in it. Anything could happen in surgery. As Brian had said, her father was older, less hardy than someone a decade or two younger. And he'd lost so much blood. If she closed her eyes, she could see it, oozing out onto the floor, bubbling up between Tristan's fingers.

Marti gagged, then sat up, letting her head drop down to her knees.

She barely heard the door when it opened, and didn't bother to look up to greet her visitor. A nurse, probably. Or a doctor. Or Brian, back to tell her something else she didn't want to hear.

"Hey, babe. How are you holding up?" Tristan's voice should have pulled her from the fog she was in, made her leap from the bed and rush forward to demand answers, but she couldn't make herself look up, let alone stand. She was afraid. Afraid of what she might see in his face and in his eyes.

The mattress dipped under his weight as he sat beside her. Close. So close she could feel the cold chill of fall that he'd carried in. He brushed hair from her neck, his hand sliding across her skin.

"Sunshine?" He pulled her in, wrapping her in autumn mist and strength. "Your dad is out of surgery. He's alive."

At his words the tension that held her upright seeped out, and she sagged against him, her arms wrapping around his waist, her face buried against his shoulder. She wanted to ask questions, but her body shook with fatigue, with relief, with fear that still thrummed through her, and she couldn't get the words out.

"It's okay. Everything is going to be okay." Tristan smoothed her hair, pressed her closer to his chest. She could feel his heart beat, the steady rhythm clashing with her frantic pulse. The tears she'd been trying so hard to hold at bay escaped, rolling down her cheeks, spilling onto Tristan's shirt. She let them fall, too drained to wipe them away. Her father was alive. For now, that was all she would think about. For now, that would have to be enough.

FIFTEEN

Tristan grabbed a blanket from the end of the bed and pulled it around Martha's shoulders, wishing he could offer her more.

He couldn't give her what he wanted—a promise that her father would live and that he'd fully recover. The doctors were giving Jesse Gabler a forty percent chance of survival. But doctors didn't know everything. Only God could determine whether the man would live or die.

"How bad is he?" Martha lifted her head, looking at him for the first time since he'd entered the room. Her face was stark white in the darkness, her eyes feverishly bright.

"He's bad, Sunshine, but not so bad that he can't survive."

"But will he?" She straightened, tugging the blanket close around her chest. She looked young, vulnerable and scared. If he could have, he would have hidden the truth from her, let her think for just a little while that the picture wasn't as grim as doctors were painting it. But he couldn't. No matter how young Martha looked, she was an adult. She had the right to know the truth.

"The doctors are giving him a forty percent chance of making it."

She nodded, let the blanket drop and stood. "That's better than I thought. I'm going to see him."

She took a step away, her movements unsteady enough to make Tristan wonder just how far she'd be able to go.

He jumped up, wrapping his good arm around her waist and adding his support to her trembling legs. "Slow down, babe. You're not going anywhere if you end up on the floor."

"So you're not going to tell me I can't go?"

"He's your father. I'd never tell you that."

She offered a shaky smile. "Okay. Then maybe I'd better sit down for a minute, because things are starting to fade."

"You lost a lot of blood." Too much blood. On Martha. Jesse. The floor. The walls. Everywhere. Because Tristan hadn't thought Johnson would be so brazen. Because he hadn't been careful enough.

Tristan pushed the thoughts away. He needed to focus on the present, not obsess on the past and its mistakes. He helped Martha sit down, poured water from a plastic carafe on the bedside table and held the cup out to her, letting himself think only of now. This moment. Making sure Martha was okay. "Drink this. I'm going to find a wheelchair."

His tone was harsher than he'd intended, and Martha grabbed his hand, holding him in place when he would have walked away. "It wasn't your fault, you know."

Surprised that she'd read him so easily, he squeezed her fingers. "I was there to protect you. I failed. In the process I nearly got your father killed."

"It *wasn't* your fault."

"Sunshine—"

"Don't say it. Don't say that you should have been more careful, or you should have known that Johnson would be there, or that you could have prevented what happened. Because if it's true about you, it's just as true about me. I knew Johnson was a killer. I never should have let Dad come near me. If this is your fault, then we share the blame equally." She looked away as she spoke, and he knew that she believed what she was saying.

"You couldn't have known, and so you couldn't have prevented it."

"Then neither could you." She took a deep, shuddering breath that tore at Tristan's heart. He wanted to make things right. Wanted to be an epic hero, a man who could defeat every monster, even those that couldn't be seen. Like worry. Like fear. Like guilt and self-blame.

He caught her tear with his thumb, wiping it away, his pulse leaping at the contact. He wasn't sure how he felt about that. For years, he'd avoided serious relationships. He'd known too many ATF agents whose marriages had crumbled under the strain of long work hours and uncertain futures. He'd always thought it better to be alone than to risk creating something that wouldn't last. He never went out with a woman more than three times. Any more than that and he risked falling into something he absolutely wanted to avoid.

Lately, though, reassessing his relationship rules seemed like a good idea. Lately, forever seemed like it might just be a possibility. Martha's strength, her independence, her optimism and faith reminded him that as many women as there were who couldn't handle being with a man whose job demanded so much, there were just as many who could.

And only one that he might be willing to try it with.

He forced the thought to the back of his mind, and let his hand fall away from Martha's cheek. "I'll be back with the wheelchair in a minute."

She nodded, but didn't speak. He couldn't blame her. It was nearly four in the morning. If she was feeling as tired as he was, she was probably too exhausted to speak. He did his best to be quick as he found the wheelchair and a nurse who gave him permission to use it. Then he informed the officer on guard duty that Martha was leaving.

Tristan had already spoken to his boss, arranged a safe house for her to stay in until Johnson was caught. There would be no more chances taken. No more opportunities for Johnson to silence Martha.

Now all he needed to do was get Martha out of the hospital under Johnson's radar. He pulled his cell phone out and dialed Grayson's number, relieved when he heard his brother's harsh greeting.

"What?"

"I've got a problem and I need your help."

"At four in the morning?"

"It's a big one."

"Tell me."

"I'm at Lakeview Memorial. Martha and her father were shot last night."

"How come I didn't hear about this?" Grayson's harsh grumble had been replaced by cold, precise questions. He was in lawyer mode—logical, savvy. Someone Tristan needed on his team.

"We're keeping it quiet. Trying to keep as much information out of Johnson's hands as possible, but I'm not convinced that's kept him from finding her here."

"What do you need me to do?"

"Do you know the all-night convenience store a block west of the hospital?"

"Yeah."

"I need you to meet me there. Martha's father is in bad shape. He's at the Lynchburg trauma center."

"You want me to give you a ride?"

"I do, but it could be dangerous. You need to know that ahead of time."

"And?"

"And there's a potential that someone could get hurt."

"When isn't there? Give me fifteen minutes, and I'll be there." Grayson hung up in typical Grayson style, quickly with no goodbye. As if he didn't have time to waste on such things.

This time, he didn't. They had to move fast. Keep one step ahead of Johnson.

Tristan strode back to Martha's room, expecting to find her seated on the bed just where he'd left her.

Why he'd expected that, he didn't know.

Since he'd met her there hadn't been one time when she'd stayed where he'd asked her to. This time wasn't any different. Instead of sitting meekly on the bed, she was hovering in the doorway, staring down the police officer assigned to guard her as he blocked her path to the hallway.

He stepped aside as Tristan approached, and Martha moved into the hallway dressed in the same dark jeans she'd been wearing earlier, her shirt replaced by a hospital gown. Thick bandages peeked out from beneath the short sleeve of the gown and blood stained her hands.

Had she noticed?

"I thought you were never coming back."

"I tried to be quick. Sit down before you fall down." He took her elbow, urging her into the chair. She was still trembling, but not as violently. Dark crescents shadowed her eyes and her skin was colorless, her lips as pale as her cheeks, her freckles dark specks on white canvas.

Despite that, she looked ready to fight, ready to face whatever would come. "I'm sitting. So, let's go."

"I'll push her." The officer stepped forward. "Which direction?"

"We'll take the service elevator to the basement and go out the delivery bay. I've arranged transportation."

It didn't take long to make it down to the basement. Getting outside took a little longer. Undercover officers searched the perimeter of the building and cleared it before they called for Tristan to move out. He borrowed a heavy jacket from a housekeeper, helped Martha ease her arms into it. Then accepted a jacket the officer who'd accompanied them held out.

He pulled it on, covering his cast. "Thanks for your help. Do you mind bringing the wheelchair back up?"

The officer shook his head. "Not at all. You planning on coming back here tonight?"

No, but that was need-to-know information, and as much as the officer had helped, Martha's whereabouts and schedule were things he didn't need to know. "I'm not sure. We'll call your office if we do."

"Good. You have a good day." The officer wheeled the chair away and disappeared from view.

"Can we go now?" Martha shifted impatiently. Obviously, she was as anxious as Tristan to be on their way. No doubt the same clock that was ticking the minutes away in Tristan's head was ticking in hers.

"If you're ready."

"I've been ready." Martha looked determined, but there was no mistaking the fear in her eyes.

"We don't have to do this, Sunshine. Sue is with your dad. He's not alone. If you don't want to—"

"I said, I'm ready. Is our ride right outside?"

"Johnson will be expecting you to catch a ride from here if you leave. My brother is waiting a block away."

"A block." She straightened her spine, lifted her chin and nodded. "I can make it."

"I knew you'd say that. You're tougher than most of the men I know."

"If that's a compliment, thank you. If it's not, I don't want to know." She smiled, pulling the hood of the jacket over her hair. Her curls peeked out from underneath, brushing against her cheek and neck. Despite her fatigue, she looked beautiful, her eyes gold-green fire.

"It's definitely a compliment." He leaned toward her, knowing he shouldn't do it. Telling himself it wasn't the time or the place. Ignoring his own advice as he inhaled the antiseptic hospital scent that clung to Martha and the more subtle scent of chocolate that was like coming home.

Her eyes widened as his lips brushed hers.

Warm silk.

Sweet honey.

Promises.

He meant the kiss to be brief, but it lingered, the world fading…then coming into sharp focus as footsteps sounded somewhere behind them. He jerked back, glancing over his shoulder. A janitor pushed a cart into a storage closet, then moved away.

"We'd better go." Martha spoke quietly, and Tristan turned back to face her.

She looked the way he felt—surprised.

Worried.

Intrigued.

There was something between them. Something he hadn't expected, but that he wouldn't deny.

Possibilities.

He shouldn't want to explore them, but he did.

There was a reason for that, he thought. God didn't bring people into each other's lives without a purpose. He and Martha had met during difficult circumstances, but circumstances changed and eventually Tristan would have time to decide what direction he wanted their relationship to go. If it was going to go anywhere.

And he had a feeling it was.

He pushed open the service door and led Martha out into the cold, dark morning.

SIXTEEN

Grayson Sinclair was nothing like Tristan and everything like him. Both men were tall, broad-shouldered and handsome, but if Tristan was fire, Grayson was ice. While Tristan moved with a lithe and deadly grace, Grayson's movements were sharp, precise and to the point as he ushered Martha into the backseat of his dark sedan, and then turned to his brother. "Glad you finally showed up. I was beginning to think I'd have to come running to rescue you."

"When have you ever had to do that?" Tristan settled into the seat beside Martha, his large frame taking up more than its fair share of space. Or maybe it just felt that way because Martha was so aware of him. His short hair mussed, his chin shadowed with the beginnings of a beard, he looked tough, even dangerous, yet sitting next to him made Martha feel safer than she'd felt all night. She shoved the thought to the back of her mind. Later, she'd pull it out and examine it more closely. For now, all she could think about was getting to her father's side. Everything else was secondary to that.

"I could name a few, but I wouldn't want to embarrass you in front of your friend." Grayson slid in behind the steering wheel, meeting Martha's eyes in the rearview mirror, his expression somber. "Since I was just sitting twiddling my thumbs waiting for my slowpoke brother, I decided to make good use of my time. I called the hospital to check on your dad."

At his words, Martha tensed, her heart jumping with anxiety. At any second she expected to hear the news that her father had passed away. The moment he'd been shot had been replaying in her mind for hours. All that blood. Her father's blood. His sunken eyes. His labored breath.

Don't miss me too much, doll.

The words echoed in her head, but she shoved them away, not wanting to think that he might have been saying goodbye forever. "How is he?"

"Holding his own."

That seemed like a catchphrase for "he's alive for now, but may not be for long." "Did they say if he's awake?"

"Sorry. I was lucky to get that much information out of them." He pulled out onto the nearly empty road, the car picking up speed, but not going nearly fast enough for Martha's taste. She wasn't one to break traffic laws, but in this instance ten or fifteen or twenty miles an hour above the speed limit didn't seem like such a bad thing.

Twenty miles. That's how far it was to the hospital. Martha had been there enough times to know they should be there in a half hour.

Not long.

Still, it seemed like an eternity. Anything could happen in that amount of time. Her father's heart could stop. He could have a stroke, a blood clot, or simply slip quietly from this world into the next. Worse, Gordon Johnson could find his way into his room and finish what he'd started.

Her hands clenched at the thought, her fingers curling into tight fists. Of course, Johnson wouldn't go after her father.

Why would he? It was Martha he wanted to get rid of. But what if he did? What if he tried to kidnap Dad to get Martha to cooperate and killed him in the process? What if—

"Relax. We'll be there soon." Tristan covered her hand with his, gently prying open her fingers and smoothing his thumbs over the crescent-shaped gouges on her palms. Something shivered to life inside her. Something she acknowledged even as she shoved it to the farthest reaches of her mind.

"I just hope *soon* is soon enough."

"Lynchburg General is a good hospital with an outstanding trauma team. They'll do everything they can for your father. He's in good hands." Grayson cut into the conversation, his smooth tenor very different from his brother's gritty baritone.

"I know, but I can't help worrying. Dad's not as young as he used to be."

"But he's tough. Strong. In good shape for his age." Tristan squeezed her hand, offering comfort that Martha shouldn't want. Hadn't she just been telling herself that she didn't need a man in her life? That she was perfectly capable of going it alone? That the only person she needed to depend on was herself?

Of course she had. Yet here she was, allowing Tristan to take care of her, to hold her hand, to offer comfort. Alarm bells should be shrieking inside her, screaming that the barriers around her heart were being breached. Instead, all she heard was the sluggish throb of her pulse and the grinding worry in her stomach.

Oh, yeah. She also heard her brain telling her that if she was going to depend on a guy, Tristan was the kind of guy she could depend on. The *only* guy she'd want to depend on.

Not good, but Martha was too tired and too worried to think about it, or to pull her hand away from his, or to even pretend

that she didn't need him sitting beside her telling her everything was going to be okay.

"When I was a kid, I thought my dad could do anything.
Leap over buildings, outrun bullets, stop a speeding train. It
didn't take me long to realize he couldn't actually do all those
things, but in my mind he was still invincible." She spoke
quietly, sharing with Tristan in a way she never had with Brian.

"I guess most kids think that about their parents."

"I guess they do." She smiled, remembering the hikes she
and her dad had been on, the camping trips, the hours spent
working in his store. "With Dad and me, though, everything
was a team effort. There couldn't be one of us without the
other. Where he went, I went. To his store, on hunting trips,
hiking, camping, fishing. Now that he's getting older, I realize
our time together is limited. I accept that, but I guess I'm just
not ready to say goodbye."

"You're not going to have to, Sunshine. God didn't save your
father's life on the operating table so He could take it in the ICU."

"I want to believe that, but no matter how much I trust that
God is in control and that He'll work everything out, I also
know that bad things can happen. They *do* happen. I'm not
immune to them. None of us are."

"That doesn't mean they'll happen this time."

"It doesn't. It also doesn't mean they won't. I need to be
prepared for that."

"There's no doubt in my mind that whatever happens,
you'll handle it. You're a strong woman, Martha. It's one of
the things I admire about you. When things get tough, that's
when you shine. And you'll shine this time. No matter what."

No matter what. No matter if her father lived or died. No
matter if Johnson came after Martha again. She'd be fine. She
really wanted to believe Tristan was right, and that she'd hold

up under whatever trouble came her way. She wanted to believe it, but she felt shaky, unsure. As if the world had tilted and she'd tilted with it. Off balance, she couldn't quite grasp the determination that usually brought her through tough situations.

She sighed, leaning her head back against the seat, Tristan's finger still linked with hers, his hand anchoring her. To reality. To hope. To the faith that suddenly seemed as elusive as a dream.

What do You want me to learn from this, Lord? There must be something. Some life lesson that will hurt, but that will help my faith grow.

The prayer whispered through her mind, but Martha felt no peace. Eventually, she'd be able to look back and see things clearly, but right now everything that had happened in the past few days seemed surreal and confusing. No matter how hard she tried, she couldn't quite wrap her mind around the fact that someone wanted her dead. Dead! And that in trying to kill her, that man had almost killed her father.

"We're here. Want me to pull up in front of the main entrance?" Grayson's words broke the silence, pulling Martha from her circling thoughts.

"Drive around the back. I've got some people waiting to make sure we get inside safely."

"You think Johnson is going to show up here?" If Grayson was worried by the thought, his tone didn't show it. He sounded as relaxed and untroubled as he had when they'd been introduced.

"Not if he thinks Martha is still at Lakeview Memorial. Since there's no guarantee he does, I'm erring on the side of caution."

"I taught you well, little brother."

"Little? Last time I checked, I was an inch taller than you."

The banter between brothers continued as Grayson drove to the back of the building. Several police cars were parked there, angled close to the hospital, but Martha knew they'd be a flimsy barrier against a barrage of bullets. And it wasn't like there weren't plenty of places for Johnson to take aim from. A parking garage hulked above the back lot, three stories tall and dark despite numerous lights. A great place for a killer to stay hidden until he was ready to make his move.

Uniformed officers were stationed near a back door, their faces shadowed by hats, their guns in holsters at their waists. It looked like a scene out of an action flick, but it was real. Too real.

Martha's stomach clenched, her breath catching in her throat as Grayson stopped the car. The engine died, the silence deafening.

Open the door, Marti. Get out of the car. Go in the building. Find your father.

But no matter how many times the words raced through her mind, Martha couldn't seem to move. She was frozen in place, her fear sapping her strength, stealing her ability to move.

Gunshots.

Blood.

Death just a heartbeat away.

Did she really want to step outside and live it all again?

An officer pulled open her door, several others standing beside him, forming a wall of protection that looked even less effective than the police cars. "Ms. Gabler? If you're ready to go in, we've cleared everything for you to go up and see your father."

Cleared everything with the doctors, or cleared the halls to make sure Johnson wasn't lurking somewhere? Martha's mouth was too dry to ask, and instead of taking the officer's hand and allowing him to pull her from the car, she stayed put, her mind screaming for her to grab the door and slam it shut.

"You're not chickening out on me, are you, Sunshine?" Tristan whispered in her ear, his words spurring her to action.

"No." She took the officer's hand, and was pulled out into the cold morning air. Several pairs of eyes watched as she took a shaky step away from the car. Could they see how scared she was?

She felt dizzy, her ears buzzing, her heart slushing through her veins but apparently not bringing much oxygen to her brain. If she collapsed, one of the officers would feel obligated to catch her. That would be bad. She really needed to lose a few pounds before some poor guy had to lift her off the pavement. The inane thought ran through her mind as she swayed, stars dancing in front of her eyes. Apparently, she'd lost more blood than she should have, because no matter how hard she tried, she couldn't quite keep the world steady beneath her feet.

"Are you okay?" Tristan wrapped an arm around her waist, saving her from doing a face-plant onto the ground, and saving his friends from having to peel her off it. Then again, maybe he was saving himself. One arm or not, Martha had a feeling he'd be the first to attempt to hoist her up if she went down.

Which she was not going to do.

She'd lost a little blood. Big deal. People lost blood all the time. Her father was in the hospital. She was going to walk in on her own two feet and see him. Nothing could keep her from doing that. Not Gordon Johnson and not a pint or so of lost blood.

"Martha?" Tristan stopped walking and looked down into her eyes, concern etching fine lines near the corners of his eyes. "Do you want me to have someone get a wheelchair for you?"

"No way. I'm right as rain." Kind of.

"You're sure?"

"Of course I'm sure." To prove her point she took a quick step forward and felt the earth tilt again, this time too far. And she tilted with it, falling into blackness as the world disappeared.

SEVENTEEN

Tristan paced the hall outside the room where they'd brought Martha twenty minutes earlier, adrenaline humming through him and begging for release. Despite nearly twenty-four hours without sleep, he wasn't tired. Instead, he felt wound up, energized. Ready to go. In other circumstances, he'd be out on the hunt, searching for Johnson, knowing he was close and not giving up until they were face-to-face. But these weren't other circumstances, and his need to find Johnson was outweighed by his need to make sure Martha and her father were okay. It hadn't been a good night for the Gabler family. Tristan intended to do everything in his power to make sure the new day was a better one.

"Is Martha okay? One of the nurses told me they had to bring her in on a stretcher. I should have found a ride to Lakeview General while Jesse was in surgery. Martha shouldn't have gone through all this alone. It was too much for her." Sue hurried down the hall toward him, her words spilling out in frantic staccato beats, her round face creased with time and worry.

Hours ago, she'd seemed vibrant and lively. Now she was drained, her face gray and worn. Grief stole life as brutally as any disease. Tristan had seen it enough to know that for sure.

"It wasn't too much for her, Sue, and she wouldn't have wanted you to leave Jesse here alone."

"I hope you're right. I really do. Jesse and I haven't been married long, and I want so badly to be the mother that Martha never had. What if she thinks I was wrong to stay here, or expected me to come with her? What if she's angry with me and we never speak again? These things happen all the time, Tristan. They do. I've seen it on *Oprah*."

Tristan put a hand on her shoulder, hoping to stop the flow of words. "They're not going to happen this time. Martha isn't that kind of person. Besides, I know for a fact that she was relieved to have you here with her father. How is he doing, by the way?" Refocus her thoughts. Make her talk about something else. That was the goal, though Tristan wasn't sure he'd be successful. Sue was a great lady, but he had a feeling that refocusing her attention wasn't always easy.

"The same. He still hasn't opened his eyes. When he finally does, I'm going to have a thing or two to say about how badly he scared me." Despite the upbeat words, her eyes were red from tears, her lips trembling as if she was holding in much greater emotion.

"Sometimes it takes a while for a patient to come out of the anesthesia completely."

"That's what the doctors are telling me, but it doesn't make me feel much better." She paused, wiping away a tear that slid down her cheek. "He looks bad. Really bad."

"Tomorrow, he'll look better."

"The doctors told me that, too." She sighed and knocked on the door to Martha's room.

The door swung open, and Tristan was relieved to see Martha lying on a bed, her wild curls spiraling in every direction, her eyes flashing green-gold fire. She looked ready to do battle, which was a whole letter better than how she'd looked when she'd nearly collapsed at his feet. "Tristan, please tell the nurse that I am perfectly capable of going to see my father in the ICU."

"Please tell Ms. Gabler that this isn't about being capable. This is about common sense. The last thing her father needs is for his daughter to pass out while she's visiting him." The nurse who'd opened the door looked dour and disapproving, her eyes bright with irritation as she speared Tristan with a look meant to force cooperation.

Too bad he wasn't in the mood to cooperate.

No matter how much he wanted to believe Jesse would be okay, he couldn't be sure what the next few hours would bring. If Martha didn't see her father now, she might never see him alive again. No way would he be part of letting that happen. "She's come all the way from Lakeview General to be with her father. I'm sure we can find a way to get her into his room without her passing out again."

"I do understand the situation. I know she wants to see her father, but he's not conscious yet, so I really think it's best if Martha rests for a few hours before we bring her upstairs."

"What if her father doesn't have a few hours left?" He spoke quietly, knowing Martha and Sue were listening, but not willing to sugarcoat the truth of the situation.

The nurse's lips tightened, her scowl deepening, but she nodded. "All right. I'll get a wheelchair and we'll take her to ICU, but when she's done there, she's to come directly back to her room. The doctor wants her admitted. If her blood count doesn't come up, we may need to do a transfusion."

A transfusion? It was Tristan's turn to scowl. Obviously, Martha had lost more blood than he'd realized. There'd been plenty of it on the floor at her house, plenty of it on him. He'd assumed most of it was Jesse's, and had focused on that. Solve the bigger, more deadly problem first. Then take care of the less dangerous situation. It had been a knee-jerk reaction born of training and years of facing tough multifaceted problems. But even while he'd tended to Jesse, his mind had been shouting that he should be helping Martha.

"Hey! I'm right here, guys. I can speak for myself, or at least participate in the conversation," Martha said as she eased to the edge of the bed, placing her feet on the floor and looking as if she had every intention of getting up and walking to the door.

"I wouldn't do that if I were you, Sunshine. You end up on the floor, and there will be no way you'll be able to convince anyone that you're strong enough to see your dad."

She frowned, but didn't make any more effort to stand.

"Martha! Thank goodness you're okay!" Sue rushed forward as the nurse left the room, throwing her arms around Martha and hugging her vigorously.

Tristan gave the two women a few minutes to discuss Jesse's injuries and prognosis before doing what he'd been wanting to all along—move toward the bed.

Martha smiled as he approached, a sweet, gentle curve of her lips that welcomed him into her circle of family, her hair curling softly around her face, begging him to touch the silky strands. He shouldn't. There were too many other things he should be doing. Like checking in with his boss, making sure there were men stationed at both hospitals ready to bring Johnson in if he should dare to show his face.

"You're looking grim, Tristan."

"It's been a grim night. How are you feeling?"

"Dandy."

"You're not in any pain?"

"If I am, it's completely overshadowed by the pain of embarrassment I'm feeling."

"What's to be embarrassed about?" He gave in to temptation and lifted a heavy lock of her hair, letting it slide through his fingers, the smooth texture feeling like the finest silk against his callused skin.

"I passed out in front of a bunch of strangers and had to be scraped off the pavement. What's not to be embarrassed about?"

Tristan couldn't help chuckling. "You didn't exactly fall onto the pavement, so no scraping was required."

"Someone caught me before I fell?"

"Yes." *He* had, but he doubted Martha wanted details. Her independent nature was one of her greatest gifts, but also one of her most serious weaknesses. To be tough, a person had to be willing to be weak. He doubted Martha had learned to do that yet.

"Even worse."

"You'd rather have ended up on the ground?"

"I'd rather it not have happened at all."

"Your ride is here." The nurse stepped back into the room, pushing a wheelchair in front of her.

"Thank you." Martha eased into the chair, biting her lip as the nurse pushed her out into the hall. She was anxious. Tristan could see it in the way she clenched her fists and sat stiffly in the chair. He wanted to reach out and squeeze her shoulder, offer her silent support, but the nurse was moving away, taking her toward the bank of elevators at the far end of the hall with short, quick steps that refused interference.

Probably she wanted Tristan and Sue to stay in Martha's room and wait for their return. She was going to be disappointed. No way was Tristan going to let Martha out of his sight again. The police might be on the ball, making sure that

Johnson wouldn't get into the hospital and get to Martha, but Tristan wasn't leaving her safety to someone else. He'd already failed her and her father once. He didn't plan to do it again.

The nurse shot him a look as he and Sue stepped onto the elevator, but she didn't tell him to return to the room. Not that he would have listened if she had.

He leaned his shoulder against the wall as the nurse gave Martha instructions. "As you know, your father is quite weak. He's hooked up to a lot of machines, and he's unconscious. That doesn't mean he can't hear you. When you go in to see him, make sure you talk to him and let him know you're there."

"All right."

"Don't be nervous about what you see. The machines are serving a vital purpose." The nurse pushed Martha out onto the third level of the building and headed in the direction of a large sign that pointed out the ICU.

"I understand."

"Good. Some family members get a little panicky when they see someone they love hooked up to monitors and machines."

"I'm not the panicky type."

"Then you'll be just fine. Just talk calmly to your dad, tell him he's going to be fine. When your time is up, I'll come in and get you to bring you back to your room. Please don't try to get down there on your own."

"I won't. When do you think my father will regain consciousness?"

"No one can say. I know it's hard to do, but in situations like this, the best thing is to just take it a day at a time and be there for your dad." For the first time since the door to Martha's room had opened, the nurse looked compassionate and kind.

"I will. Thank you."

"You can only visit for ten minutes every half hour. And

only one at a time, so I'm afraid you and your mother will have to take turns."

At the word *mother* Martha stiffened, but she didn't correct the mistake. Neither did Sue. It seemed there was an unspoken understanding that in this situation, they were family. No matter how new the relationship or fragile the bond.

"I understand." Martha glanced at Sue, then Tristan, her eyes filled with a million worries. Tristan wanted to tell her everything was going to be fine, that her dad would be up and around sooner than she imagined, and that Johnson would be behind bars before she stepped out of the hospital again. But there were no guarantees in life, and no matter how badly he wanted those things to be true, he knew that only time would tell for certain.

"Here we are. You two can wait in our lounge while Martha visits her dad." The nurse pointed to a door that led off the hallway. Tristan hesitated. He knew what he'd find inside— grief. Thick. Hard. Ugly.

He'd been there before. In rooms just like that one. Faced family members of fallen agents and seen the ravages of grief, the horror of loss. He'd rather stand eye to eye with a hundred cold-blooded killers than see one mother crying over her wounded child, one wife grieving for a husband she had to let go, one husband trying to comfort his children. That's what he worked so hard for. Get the bad guys off the street so that fewer people had to deal with the horror of losing someone they loved. It was another reason he'd never committed to a relationship. Never considered marriage, kids, family. He didn't want his wife, his kids, sitting in a room like that one, waiting, wondering. Crying.

No, he did not want to go into that room and see the harsh

side of life. The alternative, though, was leaving Martha on the third floor and waiting down in her room for her return. That wasn't an option, so he took a deep breath, braced himself and stepped into the maelstrom of emotion.

EIGHTEEN

Martha had expected her father to look bad. She thought she'd braced herself for it, but seeing him lying in bed, tubes and wires snaking around him, was harder than she'd imagined. The nurse wheeled her close, positioning the wheelchair at the head of the bed, so that Martha could reach out and touch his leathery cheek.

"Dad, it's Martha. Can you hear me? Sorry it took me so long to get here, but you know what they say—better late than never. I've been praying for you, and Tristan is doing everything he can to get the guy who did this."

"That's exactly what you need to do, Martha." The nurse spoke briskly as Martha took her father's limp hand in hers. "Just talk to him like it's any other day."

Any other day? Any other nightmare was more like it. Martha's hand shook as she brushed it over her father's wiry hair. He looked shrunken, older than his seventy years, all his vibrancy, all his life gone.

Please don't let it be gone.

"Will you be okay in here on your own? Is there anything I can get you?" Nurse Ratched hovered near the door, watching with a worried expression. The first one Martha had seen from her since she'd arrived. Maybe she'd pegged the nurse all wrong. Maybe the woman wasn't a brute who loved throwing her weight around. Maybe she really was concerned about Martha's well-being.

"Martha?" Apparently, she'd taken too long to answer. The nurse was moving toward her again, looking as if she was ready to wheel Martha out into the hall.

"I'm fine. I don't need anything. Unless…" She stopped herself before she could say what she'd been thinking.

"What?"

Don't say it, Martha. You don't need Tristan in here with you. You're fine on your own. You're independent. Strong. Able to face whatever may come on your own.

"Would it be okay if Tristan came in here with me? My friend who brought me in, I mean."

Way to listen to your own advice.

"I'm sorry. The rules—"

"I know. It's okay. I'm fine."

The nurse eyed her for a moment, then nodded and stepped into the hall. It was for the best. Martha really didn't want Tristan with her. Okay. She did. But she didn't *want* to want him with her. That had to count for something.

She brushed a hand against her father's cheek, feeling the dry warmth of his skin. He'd always seemed so young. Now he looked like an aged husk of the person he'd once been. How could it be that a man who'd been so filled with life could suddenly be so close to death?

One moment.

One heartbeat of time.

That was all it had taken.

And all it would take for him to drift out of her reach. "Dad, if you can hear me, I want you to know how much I love you. I know it wasn't easy raising me alone, but you did a great job."

Her voice broke on the words, tears slipping down her

cheeks. This was her fault. All her fault. If she hadn't gone into the mountains to nurse her pride, if she hadn't dated a man who'd been so obviously wrong for her, if she hadn't wanted so much more out of life than what she had, then her father would still be fine.

The soft click of the door told her someone had entered the room. Probably the nurse coming to check on her. She didn't look up, just kept her eyes trained on her father, hoping her tears were hidden by the hair that fell across her cheek.

Someone touched the back of her head, wove fingers through her hair and let them rest at the base of her skull, the touch soft as a butterfly's kiss.

Her heart leaped in acknowledgment even before Tristan spoke.

"Everything will be okay." His words washed over her, his hand lifting, then smoothing down her cheek to brush her tears away.

She didn't resist as he tugged her to her feet and wrapped her in his arms, his hand pressing against her back, his summer-blue eyes probing hers. "The nurse said you wanted me in here with you."

"She told me it was against the rules."

"I guess she decided she could bend them for once."

"Dad looks terrible."

"I know."

"It's all my fault."

"Not even close."

"It is. I was such an idiot. Dating Brian when everyone told me how arrogant and self-serving he was. If I'd listened to them, Dad wouldn't be here right now."

"Weren't you just telling me that I couldn't have known what would happen? That I couldn't have prevented it?"

"That's different."

· "Because it's me and not you?" He sighed, his breath ruffling her hair. "I've been thinking about this a lot the last few hours. Sometimes things happen in a way no one can predict or prevent. If we could both go back and make different decisions to change the outcome, we would—but we can't. So we've just got to hold on tight and pray that when we get to the end of the journey, we'll understand why things happened the way they did."

He was right. Marti's head knew it, but her heart was telling her something different. Her heart was telling her that she could have saved her father a lot of pain and trauma if she'd made better choices.

As if sensing her thoughts, Tristan tugged her even closer, pressing her head to his chest, his warmth, his strength, easing the icy fear that ran through Martha's veins.

She should put some distance between them, tell him that she was okay and didn't need his support, but she didn't. Her arms wound around his waist, her hands fisted in his shirt as her entire body shouted that she was exactly where she was supposed to be.

And the truth hit her like a ton of bricks.

She needed Tristan. *Needed* him. Not like she'd needed Brian—as a means to an end, a way to get one step closer to the family she'd always longed for. With Tristan, it was different. It was the kind of need that said—when you're with me, the world is a better place. When you're with me, I'm not alone anymore. When you're with me, all I want is for you to stay.

The kind of need that made a person vulnerable.

The kind of need she'd never, ever imagined she'd feel.

This was bad. Really, really bad.

She stepped away, avoiding Tristan's eyes, not wanting

him to see what she was feeling. "How is Sue holding up? I didn't even think to ask her."

"She's doing okay. One of her sons is flying in to stay with her. He'll be here in the morning."

Martha nodded, putting a little more distance between them as she leaned over her father and lifted his hand. "Hey, Dad, it's me again, Martha. Anytime you're ready, you can open your eyes and let me know you're in there. I'm starting to worry that you've landed on that tropical island you always dreamed about visiting and you've decided to stay."

He didn't even twitch, his gray-tinged face lifeless, his eyes closed.

"Sue is worried about you, too. Neither of us knows what we'll do if you're not up and around in time to put up the Christmas lights. Remember last year? How you decided to outdo your neighbors? There was so much light pouring off your house, Darrel James called the sheriff and complained." The memory made her smile through the tears that were falling again.

Good times. Lots of them. No matter what happened, at least she'd have those.

"It's almost time to leave, babe." Tristan spoke quietly, his words reminding her of what she'd wanted to avoid. Him. His presence. The aching need inside that said being with him was much better than being without.

"I just want to pray for him before I go." She put a hand on her father's shoulder, feeling muscle and bone. Life and strength along with fragility she hadn't noticed before. Had he always been like that and she'd just not seen it?

Tristan leaned close, his chest pressing against her back as he placed his hand over hers. There. With her. Supporting her in a way no other person ever had. Not her mother who'd run from responsibility. Not even her father who had always loved her unconditionally, but who had hurt too much when she was hurt for Martha to ever want to share all her burdens with him.

She took a deep breath, closing her eyes, forcing her mind away from Tristan and back where it belonged—with her father. "Lord, I know You're here with us, and that You're in control of the situation. I pray for Your healing hand on my father. In the same way You made the blind see and the lame walk, I pray that You'll return Dad's strength to him. I trust that Your will will be worked out in Your perfect time, and I ask for Your comfort for Sue and me as we face whatever is to come. Amen."

"Amen." Tristan's agreement rumbled out, his thumb gently caressing her knuckles as he pulled his hand away. "Ready to go back to the room?"

"Do I have a choice?" she asked, though no matter what his answer was, she knew she didn't. Her mind was fuzzy, the room swimming, colors blurring. She needed to sit down now before she fell down.

"No."

"Then I'm ready. I'll be back in a little bit, Dad. Stay strong. I love you." She leaned over, placing a kiss on his parchment skin, then straightened, blackness edging at her vision at the quick movement.

Tristan must have noticed, because he grabbed her arm, holding her steady as she sat in the wheelchair again. She felt weak. Weaker than she ever had before. As if someone had taken her energy and sucked it out, leaving her empty and wanting. Getting shot stunk.

Watching your father get shot, that was even worse.

Seeing your father lying in a hospital hooked to machines that beeped and buzzed and breathed for him, that was worst of all.

But things would get better. What choice did they have? Trouble couldn't last forever. Her father had told her that often enough. It was a motto he lived by, and one Martha had learned before she could read.

All she had to do was keep her chin up, keep believing that God was in control and keep hoping that no matter what the next day brought, He'd get her through it.

That's all she had to do, but right now, as Tristan wheeled her out of the ICU, it felt like a lot more than she could handle.

NINETEEN

Martha didn't plan to sleep when she returned to her room. She had too much on her mind. When Tristan stepped into the hall to make a phone call, she leaned back against the hospital pillows and tried to make a mental list of things she needed to get done. Call the church and put Dad on the prayer list. Get someone to feed Sue's cat. Call a cleaning company who specialized in removing bloodstains.

That one made her shudder.

What else?

Call work. Let them know she wouldn't be in for a day or two. Find out who her father's doctor was and discuss the prognosis with him. Maybe that one should be at the top of the list.

She yawned, her eyes closing despite her best efforts to keep them open. Just for a minute. That's all she needed. A minute or two of shut-eye and she'd be good as new.

Blood-red sky. Deep black clouds. Rain falling like tears. Dad, lying on cold gray stone, his eyes open, but unseeing. Johnson, gun drawn, a feral smile on his face, pointing the gun at Martha, pulling the trigger. But she wasn't the one falling with a bullet hole in her. Tristan was. Tumbling onto the ground, sprawling lifeless next to Martha's father as Johnson's laughter filled the air.

Martha jerked awake, her heart slamming in her chest, her breath heaving out as she tried to remember where she was, how she'd gotten there, what was going on.

Johnson. The hospital. Her father lying nearly lifeless in ICU.

She swung her legs over the side of the bed, wincing as her body protested the sudden movement. She felt as if she'd been run over by a truck. Every muscle in her body ached, her shoulder throbbed and she was pretty sure that things wouldn't feel any better once she was on her feet.

She was going to get to her feet, though. She didn't know how long she'd been asleep, but it was long enough that the sun streaming in through the window seemed muted, casting long shadows. According to the clock, it was just past three. She'd been sleeping for hours while her father struggled for life.

She shifted her weight, determined to ignore the pain and get up. It's what her father would have expected, and what she expected from herself.

"Going somewhere?" Tristan's voice came from behind her, and she screamed, whirling to face him.

"Tristan! I didn't realize you were here."

"Sorry about that. I didn't mean to scare you. I decided to catnap in the chair while you were sleeping. You and I both needed some rest."

"*Some* rest. I've been sleeping for hours."

"Like I said, we both needed it. With Johnson still on the loose, we've got to stay on top of our game. That means getting the rest we need."

"But my father—"

"Is being well taken care of." Tristan ran a hand down his jaw.

"I need to see him."

"I'll bring you up." He didn't even hesitate, just pushed the wheelchair to the bed, and gestured for her to take a seat.

"I don't think I need that this time. I'm feeling about two hundred times better." If she excluded the pain, and she thought she would. After all, a little pain was a lot better than being dead.

He looked as though he was going to argue, then changed his mind, shrugging broad shoulders and offering a half smile. "Suit yourself, Sunshine, but if you get halfway to your father and pass out, I'll be forced to perform a fireman's carry to get you upstairs."

"At least it would give the nurses something to talk about."

"And Brian McMath." His words were tight as he mentioned Martha's ex, his expression guarded.

"What does Brian have to do with anything?"

"He's been in here twice while you were asleep."

Ugh. That wasn't a pleasant thought. Brian McMath hanging over her while she snored the day away. Worse, Tristan sitting in a chair watching her while she snored.

Had she snored?

The thought was appalling, and Martha's cheeks heated. "Did he say what he wanted?"

"I didn't ask."

"So, what did you do, stare each other down to prove who was the most manly?"

He chuckled, his hand resting on the small of her back as they stepped out of the room. "Thanks for the laugh. I needed that."

"Did something happen while I was sleeping?"

"Something didn't happen. Johnson is still on the loose."

"Maybe he left town."

"Not Johnson. He's got a mission. He's going to follow through. Get you out of the picture so you can't testify. It might take him a day, a week or a month, but Johnson has the kind of patience that allows him to wait things out rather than rush in."

"That's not a comforting thought."

"No, but at least we can be pretty confident that he won't go into hiding until he's achieved his goal. As long as he's not in hiding, we should be able to find him."

"I guess that's going to have to be good enough."

"For now." Tristan led her to the elevator doors and pushed the button to open them. "Sue's son arrived a few hours ago. He's up in the waiting room with her, and he plans to stay until your father is released from the hospital."

"That's really good of him."

"Yeah, I'm glad he's here, since you won't be." He said it so matter-of-factly, the words almost didn't register.

When they did, Martha stiffened, turning to face him. "I *am* going to be here, Tristan. I don't know where you got the idea that I wouldn't."

"From my boss who's finally managed to arrange a safe house for you until Johnson is caught."

"You're kidding, right?"

"I wouldn't kid about something like that." The elevator door slid open again, and Tristan stepped out, grabbing Martha's arm and pulling her with him when she hesitated.

"You may not be kidding, but there is no way I'll leave this hospital until I know my father is going to be okay."

"You don't have a choice, Martha. Johnson wants you dead. He's already made that more than clear."

"We knew he wanted me dead before he tried to kill me. I don't see how last night changes anything."

"It changes plenty because now I'm not the only one who believes he's coming after you. You're a key witness in this case. No way does the ATF want to lose you."

"I don't particularly want to be lost, but I'm not leaving my father."

"Like I said, you don't have a choice." The words were final, and Martha had the feeling that no matter what she said, how she tried to argue, Tristan would say the same.

She didn't care. She'd continue to argue her point. If push came to shove, she'd simply refuse to leave the hospital.

Sure she would.

She couldn't imagine facing down Tristan, let alone the police, the ATF and whatever other government agencies might want to have a part in finding Gordon Johnson.

So she'd deal with that when the time came.

Right now, she needed to see her father and make sure he was okay.

They walked into the room, and Martha's heart sank. She didn't know what she'd been expecting or hoping for, but it wasn't what she was seeing—her father looking exactly the same as he had when she'd been in earlier. "He still doesn't look good."

"Give it time."

"How much? A day? A week? Shouldn't there be some improvement by now?" She spoke quietly as she lifted her father's hand. "Dad? Can you hear me? It's Martha again."

To her surprise, his eyes blinked open, the usual bright hazel, muted and muddy. A tube in his throat prevented him from speaking, but he squeezed her hand, his grip weak.

"Dad! You *are* in there. I was beginning to wonder. How are you feeling?"

He frowned, gesturing toward a pad of paper and pen sitting on the table next to his bed. Once she handed both to him, he wrote slowly, his hand shaking, the letters wobbly and light. Barely legible. But at least he was communicating. That had to be a good sign.

He held the paper up, and Martha squinted, trying to

make out the words. "I look awful, and you want me to go get some sleep?"

She smiled, shaking her head at her father. "I can't believe you're worried about me at a time like this."

"I'll make sure she gets the rest she needs, Jesse. You just worry about getting yourself healthy." Tristan moved smoothly into the conversation, his arm brushing hers as he leaned closer to the bed.

Martha's dad nodded, closing his eyes again. A man who'd worked hard his whole life, who could stay on his feet for twelve hours straight, tired after lifting a pen.

Martha lifted his hand again, trying to will some warmth into his cool skin. "Are you cold, Dad? Do you need another blanket?"

He didn't respond, and she squeezed gently, praying that he'd open his eyes again. "Dad?"

"Let him rest, Sunshine. He needs that more than you need him to talk." Tristan spoke quietly, and Martha knew he was right. Still, she wanted to know that he was getting better, that he was heading further away from the precipice he'd been hovering at the edge of.

"I need to speak to his doctor."

"Let's go find someone who can tell us who his doctor is."

Us.

She liked the sound of that but knew she shouldn't. Tristan was dangerous. Too much time with him and she might just start imagining that there was more to their relationship than Gordon Johnson. "Why don't you wait here with Dad in case he wakes up again. I'll go find a nurse."

"I don't think so."

"Okay, then you go. I'll stay."

"I don't think you understand the way things are going to be. Once we talk to the doctor, we're leaving here and going directly to the safe house my boss has arranged. You're staying there until Johnson is caught."

"I think you're the one who doesn't understand, Tristan. I'm an adult. I make my own decisions. And I'm deciding right now that I'm not leaving this hospital until my father is off the ventilator and close to going home."

"You made your own decisions until you walked in on a gun raid and became the state's key witness. Now things are different. You may as well get used to the idea." His eyes flashed, his jaw tight with frustration, but Martha didn't care. Short of carrying her out of the hospital, there was no way anyone from any agency was going to get her to leave.

She planned to tell Tristan exactly that, but her father made a soft noise, drawing her attention away from the argument and back to the bed.

"Hey, you're awake again. Are you—" Before she could ask if he was in pain, if he needed something, if she should go get the nurse, he gestured toward the pad of paper and pen.

As soon as she handed them to him, he scribbled a message and held it up for her to see. *Stop arguing and go.*

"You can't be serious, Dad. You were shot. You were almost killed. I'm not going to…" Her voice trailed off as he started writing again.

If something happens to you it will *kill me.*

"Nothing is going to happen to me."

Go. It will be better for both of us.

"How can it be better for both of us if you're sick and I'm off who knows where not knowing what's going on?" But it seemed her father's strength had run out. His grip on the pen slackened and it rolled onto the blanket.

"I think what your father is trying to tell you is that he'll worry too much if you don't go to the safe house. In his condition, that kind of worry is the last thing he needs." Tristan spoke into the silence, and her dad gave a subtle nod of agreement.

"You don't have to worry, Dad. I'm going to be fine."

"Because you're going to do what your father and I are suggesting, and go to the safe house." Tristan leaned past her to squeeze her father's hand. "Don't worry, Jesse, I'll take care of your daughter. Before you know it, we'll all be sitting down to another one of Sue's fine meals together."

Her father blinked twice, then closed his eyes, his face sinking in on itself. What little animation had been there was gone. If anything, he looked worse than when she'd walked in. Had she done that to him? No. No. Of course she hadn't, but Tristan was right. Her dad didn't need the extra stress that worrying about her would cause. Whether she liked it or not, the best thing she could do for him was go somewhere safe and wait things out.

And she didn't like it.

What if she went off to the safe house and he got worse? "Will I be able to call the hospital from the safe house?"

"We'll make sure you're updated on your father's condition as frequently as we are."

"We?"

"A female agent will be staying with you."

"Oh." So she wouldn't be Tristan's responsibility anymore. That was good. So why did she feel so lousy about it?

Because she was leaving her father, that was why.

And if she kept telling herself that she might start to believe it.

She leaned down and placed a kiss on her father's forehead.

"I'm going, Dad, but if you get worse I'm coming back, so you'd better just keep on getting better if you want me to stay away."

She thought he might be trying to smile as Tristan took her arm and led her out of the room.

TWENTY

The safe house wasn't anything like Martha imagined it would be. Not that she'd spent much time imagining it. She'd been too busy worrying about the doctor's guarded prognosis regarding her father's health to give anything else more than a cursory thought. Twenty miles from town, tucked away on a gravel road deep in the Blue Ridge Mountains, the house Tristan pulled up in front of was a charming villa that overlooked stunning views. Several acres of yard surrounded it, free of trees, shrubs or any other potential hiding place. Aside from that, the place didn't look any more safe than Martha's house.

"This is it?"

"Yep." Tristan stopped the engine and turned to face her. Two days without shaving had given him a rough, hard look that shouldn't have appealed to Martha. After all, she'd only ever been attracted to clean-shaven men. Men like Brian who were smooth, polished, restrained and predictable. Those were the kind of guys who were safe, easy. Tristan would never be either of those things.

Somehow that didn't seem to matter to Martha's treacherous heart. Not only did she find Tristan extremely attractive, but she was pretty sure safe and predictable would never appeal to her again. Good thing she'd decided before she'd met him that relationships weren't for her, or she might be having thoughts she shouldn't.

She cleared her throat, turning to look out the car window, avoiding Tristan's probing gaze. "It's a pretty house, but it doesn't look particularly safe."

"It's safe. Trust me on that." Tristan rounded the side of the car and pulled open her door. "Come on. Rayne has probably paced a hole through the floor already."

"Rayne is the agent who's staying with me?"

"She'll be the one you're dealing with, and she's not so good at waiting." He led her to the front door, knocked once and walked inside.

"You were supposed to be here two hours ago." A tall blonde moved across the two-story foyer. Mid-twenties. Dancer slim. Indigo-blue eyes in porcelain skin.

She was an agent?

As if she sensed Martha's doubts, Rayne met her eyes, letting her gaze drop to the bloodstained jeans and sneakers Martha wore. "You're Martha Gabler."

It wasn't a question, but Martha nodded anyway. "That's right."

"I'm Rayne Steward. I'm sorry about your dad. I know it must be hard to leave him behind."

"Thanks. It is."

"He's in good hands."

And if Martha had a dollar for every time someone had said that to her in the past twelve hours—

"But I'm sure you've heard that way too many times, so let's just get you up to your room. You're probably anxious to get cleaned up. Personally, I think a hot shower can wash away a boatload of trouble."

A shower sounded good. Great even. But Tristan would

probably leave while she was trying, without success, to wash away her problems.

She might not want to need him.

She might not want to want him around, but she did. Chalk it up to fatigue and injury, but the thought of not having Tristan close by filled her with dread. "It's okay. I can wait for a while."

"Go on, Sunshine. I've got a couple calls to make before I head out of here. Then we need to talk about the rules." Tristan nudged her toward Rayne.

"Rules?"

"Did you think I was going to leave you here without some? Who knows what kind of trouble you'd get yourself into." He smiled, and Martha wanted to throw herself into his arms, beg him not to leave her in the middle of the mountains with a stranger.

Dumb.

Really dumb.

She did not need Tristan to stay. She would not beg him to stay. She wouldn't even indicate that she wanted him to stay. She wasn't a toddler, after all. She was a grown woman, perfectly capable of taking care of herself. Hadn't she hiked into the mountains on her own just a few short days ago? Hadn't she been planning on spending a weekend completely by herself?

What had happened to the strong, independent woman she'd been?

She hadn't died, that was for sure, so there was no way Martha was going to act like a whiny, weak damsel in distress, willing to let the knight fight her battles while she hid inside the castle. She straightened her spine, stiffened her shoulders. "Just so you know, me being given rules doesn't mean I'll follow them. I need to hear what they are before I commit to them."

"You'll follow them, Martha. Otherwise how can we make sure you stay safe?" Rayne's words were calm with barely any inflection, but there was a hard edge to her tone, a sharp look in her eyes.

Definitely an agent and not a paid babysitter. And definitely someone Martha wanted to avoid crossing. For now she'd let the rule battle go. She had a feeling there'd be plenty of other things to battle over during the next few hours. Like visits to her father. Tristan might think she'd given up on the idea, but that was far from true.

She followed Rayne upstairs into a large room decorated in soft yellows. The curtains and shades were drawn, and she started to open them, stopping when Rayne put a hand on her arm.

"That's probably not the best idea." Because if Gordon Johnson is out in the wilderness with a sniper rifle you might not live to see tomorrow. Rayne didn't add the last, but Martha heard the words as clearly as if she had.

"Oh. Sorry."

"No problem. Everything in the room was brought in for you. We couldn't grab stuff from your place, but Tristan gave us sizes and color preferences. Go ahead and take a look. Make sure he got it right. You know how men are. Give them an easy job and they'll find a way to mess it up." She pulled open a dresser drawer and gestured for Martha to look inside.

Shirts, jeans, sweaters in deep purples, bright blues and vivid yellows. All in her sizes. "These look good."

"TV works. I brought a couple of old movies. Musicals. Tristan said you'd probably enjoy that more than thrillers or action flicks."

"He's right." Though how he'd known that much about her, she didn't know.

"He didn't mess that up, then. Tristan brought your purse. I left your cell phone in it, but don't use it."

"You went through my purse."

"It's what I do." She smiled, but it didn't reach her eyes. "Why don't you go ahead and check things out. Take a shower. Freshen up. Put on some clean clothes. Take your time. Tristan and I have a few things to discuss."

"All right. Thanks."

"Don't thank me. This is my job. It's what I get paid for. Just stay put until Tristan or I come up to get you, okay?"

Obviously, she wanted Martha to stay upstairs for a while. Was there some kind of secret-agent stuff that had to be discussed while she wasn't around? Some bad news Rayne didn't want her to hear?

She didn't ask. Mostly because she wasn't sure she wanted to hear the answer. She might have slept for a few hours, but she felt sick with exhaustion and pain. A shower sounded good, and she was going to take one while the taking was good, because who knew what the next few hours would bring. For all she knew, Johnson would show up here and she'd be off running through the forest trying to escape him.

Or she'd be dead.

She grimaced at the thought. "Okay."

Rayne nodded, stepped out of the room, closed the door and left Martha alone.

Silence pressed in, and she moved to the dresser, pulling out clothes. Her body was humming with nerves but dragging with fatigue. She felt drained. The truth was, she'd felt that way before Friday. It was one of the reasons she'd run to the cabin after she'd broken up with Brian. Somehow in the past few years she'd lost her focus. In pursuing her dreams, she'd forgotten to pursue her purpose.

And, she realized, those two things were not the same.

Really, would God want her to change who she was and what she believed about life and relationships so that she could have a family? Of course He wouldn't. He'd much rather she use her gifts and talents for Him. She knew that. Had always known it, but somehow the family she'd wanted, the relationship, the happy home she'd dreamed of had made her forget it for a while.

"Whatever You want my life to be, Lord. That's going to be good enough for me from now on."

An open door led to a large bathroom, its earthy tones exactly what Martha would have chosen had she been the one to decorate. Double sinks. Huge soaking tub. Separate shower. For a safe house, the place was fancy.

Martha, on the other hand, wasn't looking so hot.

She scowled at her reflection. Frizzy curly hair, dark circles under her eyes, pale skin that seemed to have taken on a greenish tinge. The jacket Tristan had borrowed for her hung over her shoulders, but didn't hide the blue hospital gown or the dirty bloodstained jeans Martha wore. Her own blood. Her father's.

Martha grimaced, running hot water into the shower so that steam filled the room and masked her reflection as she searched for something to cover the stitches in her shoulder.

Fifteen minutes later, she'd dressed in clean clothes and was running a brush through her hair, wishing she had a little makeup to liven up her pale cheeks. All her purse had yielded was a tube of Chap Stick. Oh well, at least she didn't look quite as sickly as she had before her shower. She grabbed a bottle of lotion from the sink, rubbing it into her hands, smiling a little when she realized it was chocolate scented. It didn't seem like the kind of thing Rayne would pick out. Maybe she had a soft side.

"Martha?" Tristan called through the closed bedroom door. Martha hurried to open it, her heart doing the same happy dance it did every time he was around.

"I was starting to wonder if you were going to leave without saying goodbye." The words slipped out and her cheeks heated. Why oh why had she inherited her father's fair skin?

"And miss my opportunity to remind you of the rules?"

"Remind me? You haven't told them to me yet."

"Sure I have, you've just chosen not to follow them." He smiled, pulling her out into the hallway. He'd changed into dark jeans and a navy T-shirt, and the scent of soap and shampoo clung to him. She wanted to cling to him, too, wrap her arms around his waist and beg him not to go.

Fatigue. That had to be the reason. In the two years she'd known Brian, she'd never once felt the urge to ask him to stay longer than he'd planned. "Go ahead and give me the list."

"There are only two. First one—stay inside unless Rayne is with you. Second one—do everything you're told when you're told without arguing."

"That sounds like more than two."

"Count them however you want, Sunshine, but for once, follow them. It could make the difference between living and dying. Not just for you, but for anyone protecting you."

His words were a harsh reminder that Martha wasn't at a fall retreat, that the beautiful house and awesome landscape were a temporary prison designed not just to keep her in, but to keep Gordon Johnson out. "I will."

"Promise me." He placed a hand against her cheek, staring into her eyes. For a moment she forget everything—guns, blood, death dogging her.

"I promise."

"Good." He leaned in, inhaled. "Chocolate. One of my favorite things."

"It's hand lotion. I guess Rayne picked it out."

"Actually, *I* did. In the gift shop at the hospital. I saw it and thought of the day we met. You smelled like rain and chocolate." His lips brushed hers, a second of barely-there contact that curled her toes and made her pulse race.

And then he stepped away, shooting a hard look in her direction. "Don't forget your promise."

Before she could respond, he'd moved down the steps and out the front door.

TWENTY-ONE

Three in the morning.

And she was sleepless. Again.

Martha paced the length of her room for the millionth time and scowled at the numbers glowing red on the bedside clock. She'd known that napping in the afternoon was a bad idea, but there hadn't been a whole lot else to do besides watching television, and daytime dramas really weren't her cup of tea.

What she'd really wanted was to get in a car—any car, she wasn't picky—and drive back to Lynchburg General. That hadn't been possible, not just because Rayne Steward was pacing the downstairs like a caged animal, but because she'd promised Tristan she wouldn't.

Unlike a lot of the people in her life, Martha believed in keeping her promises. Though right about now, she was thinking breaking one might not be such a bad thing.

Where was Tristan? At the hospital with her dad? Pursuing a lead that might bring him to Johnson?

Sleeping?

He'd better not be sleeping.

If she had to be awake pacing the floor, so did he.

Which, she realized, was a very selfish thought.

Unfortunately, at three in the morning, she wasn't feeling very altruistic.

The soft chime of her cell phone startled her out of her thoughts, and she rushed to her purse, grabbing the phone and staring at the caller ID. Lynchburg General. She answered without a thought, only remembering Rayne's warning not to use the phone after she was speaking into it. "Hello?"

"Martha Gabler?"

"Yes."

"This is Louise Gilmore from Lynchburg General. I've been trying to reach you for several hours. Your stepmother was finally able to remember this number."

"Is my father okay?" Martha's heart beat a sickening rhythm in her chest, her mind racing through a million things that might have gone wrong.

"I'm afraid he's taken a turn for the worse. You'll want to get here as soon as possible."

"A turn for the worse, how?"

"The doctor will explain everything, but, really, it would be for the best if you come now. He's not doing well. It may only be a matter of hours."

Hours?

She'd thought she'd have decades left with him. Now that time had been reduced to fragments of a day. She wasn't going to waste it trying to get permission to leave the safe house. She was going. Whether Rayne liked it or not. Whether Tristan liked it or not. She might be a state's witness, but she was also a daughter. She would not be denied the opportunity to say goodbye to the man who'd raised her.

Promises or no promises.

She grabbed a thick sweater from the drawer, wincing as she pulled it on over the T-shirt she wore. Her shoulder throbbed with every movement, but she worked quickly, pulling on sneakers she found in the closet. Her size exactly. Was that Tristan's doing?

Her promise to Tristan whispered through her mind as she grabbed her purse. The straightforward approach was best. Down the stairs. Out the front door. If Rayne tried to stop her, she'd just...

Well, she wasn't sure what she'd do, but she'd do something.

The hall was dark, the house silent as she hurried down the stairs. Her hand trembled as she grabbed the door knob and paused.

And then what?

She didn't have a car.

"I'm pretty sure you aren't supposed to be going outside." Rayne appeared at the top of the stairs, dressed in a black shirt and jeans, her hair pulled back from her face.

"I just got a call from the hospital. My dad isn't doing well."

"I don't think so."

"Why would I make something like that up?"

"I'm not saying you did. I'm just saying that if your dad had taken a turn for the worse, I would have already heard about it." She leaned her hip against the railing, her expression bland.

"Look, Rayne, I don't have time to argue with you about this. My dad's health is failing—"

"Who'd you talk to? What was his name?"

"Her name was Louise something. I didn't catch the last name."

"And she called your cell phone?"

"Yes."

"Let me call the hospital from the secure line. See what I can find out."

"We don't have time for that. She said my dad might only have hours left." Martha's voice broke on the words, and she pressed her lips together. The last thing she wanted to do was break down in front of Rayne.

"Look, Martha, I sympathize with what you're going through, but rushing over there before we check the situation out could be dangerous. Gordon Johnson wants you dead in a bad way. He'll go to any lengths to accomplish his goal."

"He couldn't pretend to be a woman and call me on a number he doesn't have."

"No, but he could bribe someone to help him get what he needs. I've seen it happen before. I lost a good friend that way."

"I'm sorry."

"Yeah. Me, too, and I'm not willing to risk having it happen again. Five minutes to make sure the call was on the up and up. That's not much time."

Not when you had years to play with, but when you only had hours, those five minutes seemed huge.

Martha hovered near the doorway as Rayne disappeared into a room off the foyer. Several minutes later she returned, a frown line marring her smooth forehead. "Good news and bad news. Your father is doing better, not worse. That means Johnson was trying to find you."

"Louise said she got my cell-phone number from my stepmother."

"Maybe. Maybe not. Unless we can figure out who she was, we won't know for sure."

"What now?"

"We wait for Tristan. He's on his way over."

"At three in the morning?"

"Yeah. There's been a change in plans. My boss has decided you need to go back to your father's side."

"You're kidding, right?"

"I'm afraid not. We need to bring Johnson to justice. Sooner rather than later."

"You're going to use me as bait."

"For the greater good, Martha. The longer he's on the streets, the more likely it is that someone else will get hurt. Maybe even killed."

"I don't think I like this idea."

"I don't think anyone does, but Johnson is getting antsy. He may be getting desperate. That's making the situation more and more dangerous. We need to deal with him now."

Deal with him now or spend days, weeks, maybe even months hiding from him. Martha thought she'd rather do the first. No matter how frightening it sounded. "All right."

"Don't worry. We've done this before. Most of the time, the sharks don't get the bait." She grinned, but Martha didn't think the comment was amusing.

Shark and bait? Definitely not something she wanted to dwell on. Of course she *did* dwell on it anyway, and by the time Tristan stepped into the house, her heart was galloping and she felt physically ill.

"Hey, Sunshine." He pulled her close, wrapping her in his arms. "Another long night, heh?"

"Were you at the hospital?"

"No. I was following up on a few leads. Looks like the best one just came from your cell phone." He released his hold, turning his attention to Rayne. "You talked to Sampson?"

"Yeah."

"So you know the plan."

"Bring Martha to the hospital. Give Johnson a chance to go after her."

"For the record, I'm not too fond of the plan."

"For the record, I don't think your fondness or lack thereof matters. We need to get this guy off the streets, Tristan. We need to do it now."

"Not if it means risking a civilian's life."

"We're risking civilian lives if we don't act."

"I disagree."

"You won't when he goes after Martha's father or step-mother. Or when some poor nurse or doctor is killed so he can get the old man and use him to draw Martha out."

"My dad isn't an old man."

"Sorry, I meant no offense. My point is simply that Johnson is a cold-blooded killer who is desperate to keep you from testifying against him. If that means killing a few innocent people who happen to get in his way—so be it."

"We'll get someone to fill in and pretend to be Martha."

"He may be a killer, but he's not stupid." Rayne frowned, her frustration obvious.

"I—"

"We're wasting time." Martha interrupted Tristan's words. She wanted Johnson off the streets as badly as they did, and as far as she was concerned, if going back to the hospital accomplished the goal, she'd do it. "I'm ready to go get this done."

"Do you realize how dangerous this could be?" Tristan's expression was thunderous, his eyes flashing blue fire.

"Name one thing that's happened in the past few days that hasn't been dangerous."

He scowled, pacing across the foyer. "Look, you're safe here. I want you to stay that way."

"So do I, but I also want to go back to my life. I want to be able to be there for my dad while he's recovering. I do not want to spend days, weeks or months here. I'd go crazy."

"Crazy is better than the alternative."

"We could stand here all day arguing, but it's not going to accomplish anything. I've got orders to bring Martha to the hospital." Rayne grabbed a jacket from the coat closet. "That's what I plan to do. Unless you want to do it for me."

"*You're* supposed to bring me?" Surprised, Martha turned her attention to Rayne.

"Tristan is on medical leave. He's not supposed to be doing anything more strenuous than lifting a can of soda."

"I'm taking her to the hospital."

"You sure you can handle it, Sinclair?" Rayne sent a mocking smile in his direction.

"Has there ever been any doubt about it before?"

"No, but I'm starting to think you're getting soft, and getting soft is a precursor to dying."

"Thank you, Ms. Mary Sunshine."

"Hey, I'm just saying." She paused, glanced at her watch. "Sampson will have men in place at the hospital by now. If you're taking Martha, you'd better go. If Johnson really is waiting, he'll take off if Martha doesn't get there in a reasonable amount of time."

Tristan nodded, took Martha's arm. "You ready?"

"Yes."

"Put this on under your jacket." Rayne handed her a heavy black vest. "Of course, knowing the kind of guns and weapons Johnson and Buddy have been putting out on the street, there's no guarantee that this will protect you."

Marti didn't like the sound of that, but she tugged on her vest anyway, gritting her teeth as she tried to pull the vest over her aching shoulder.

"Here—" Tristan leaned close "—let me help." His breath whispered against her hair as he eased the vest over her bad shoulder, his fingers brushing against her neck. She shivered.

"Do you think Johnson is waiting?"

"I think there's a good chance."

"Then let's go find him."

Us. The two of them together.

Despite her fear and worry, Martha couldn't help thinking that she liked the sound of that.

TWENTY-TWO

Tristan didn't like the situation. He didn't like it at all. It had been one thing to expose Martha to danger when she'd walked into his raid Friday afternoon. He'd had no choice then. Now, he did, and using her as bait to bring Gordon Johnson in was not a choice he would ever have made.

Unfortunately, it wasn't his decision, and what he liked or didn't like didn't figure into the equation. At least not as far as his boss, Daniel Sampson, was concerned. Tristan had argued with him for the fifteen minutes it had taken to drive to the safe house, but Sampson had remained unmoved. Risking one life to save hundreds, maybe even thousands, made sense. Even without Buddy, Johnson was capable of continuing to trade in illegal weapons. He had the connections, the know-how. He needed to be off the streets. Now. Not weeks or months from now.

As far as Sampson was concerned, the worst-case scenario was that Johnson would ambush Martha and kill her before they could stop him. They'd be out a witness, but there was enough manpower at the hospital to ensure Johnson's capture. Best-case scenario, one of the officers patrolling the hospital would spot Johnson before that happened. Either way, a gun-runner would be behind bars. In Sampson's mind it was a win-

win situation. And, Tristan had to cut the guy some slack, he really did believe they'd be able to keep Martha from being hurt again.

Tristan thought they could, too, but that didn't mean he liked the idea any better. Martha should be tucked away in the safe house under Rayne's watchful eye, not riding into Johnson's line of fire. His grip tightened on the steering wheel, and he wondered how many years he'd get if he kidnapped the state's key witness, took her somewhere far away and kept her there until Johnson was caught.

"Don't worry, Tristan. Everything will be fine." Martha spoke quietly, her words barely carrying over the rumbling chug of the engine.

"Aren't I supposed to be the one saying that?"

"Yeah, but seeing as how you look like you're going to tear the steering wheel to pieces, I thought I'd better say it first."

"You're something else, Sunshine."

"Something good, or something bad?"

"Definitely good." He patted her knee, some of his anxiety easing. She was right. Everything *would* be okay. He'd played out these kinds of scenarios dozens of times in the past years, and they usually ran like clockwork. There was no reason to expect this to go any differently.

"What's going to happen when we get to the hospital?" Martha sounded much calmer than Tristan felt.

"We're going to get out of the car and walk into the building like we haven't got a worry in the world."

"You don't think Johnson will realize he's being set up?"

"I do. I think that's the whole point. He's trying to get you out in the open and he doesn't care if we know it. His arrogance is going to be his undoing."

"So he's going to be waiting for me to arrive? Just waiting

there even though he knows half the state police are going to be at the hospital?" She couldn't seem to wrap her mind around it, but, then, she was a nice person, a law-abiding citizen. Someone who probably felt guilty if she went a mile an hour above the posted speed limit.

"He doesn't think he'll get caught, babe. That's the thing with men like Gordon. They've gotten away with so much, they think they can get away with anything. In the end, that's what always brings them down."

"Yeah, but how many innocent people do they bring down with them?"

"Too many. That's why my boss wants to make sure we get Johnson tonight."

"The good of the individual sacrificed for the good of the many?"

"Something like that. Only don't think of yourself as a sacrifice. You're more like a carrot held out in front of a donkey's nose. Motivation, but never meant to be eaten."

"A carrot. Make it a huge chocolate-chip cookie hanging from a treadmill, and I just might get into the imagery."

He cast a quick glance in her direction, surprised to see that she was smiling. A tense, tight smile, but it was there, her resilience carrying her through again. She'd pulled her hair into two low ponytails that fell in soft curls near her ears, and he wanted to weave his fingers through them, let the silky softness slide across his skin. Beautiful. Funny. Intelligent. She was a compelling combination. But there was something more. An indefinable something that tugged at Tristan's heart every time he was near her. No matter how much he wanted to ignore it, wanted to pretend it was nothing, the truth was that Martha was becoming part of his life. A big part. Not because she was the key to finding and capturing Johnson, but because she offered something he'd never found with another woman—a sense of belonging. As if being with Martha made him more alive, more complete.

If any of his brothers heard him say that, they'd laugh, but truth was truth. And the truth was, when he was with Martha, he felt like he was home. A strange idea, but one he hadn't been able to shake no matter how hard he'd tried.

"Sometimes I don't understand why God doesn't just reach down and fix things. You know, make life easier for us. He could. A whispered word and Johnson could be in custody without any trouble at all."

Martha's words pulled Tristan from his thoughts, and he glanced her way again. She was still smiling, but there was a sadness to it that made him wish he could take the nearest exit to wherever and hope for the best.

"It would make life easier, but I don't know if it would make things better. A placid lake is nice, but an ocean squall is a lot more interesting."

"Yeah? Well, I've had about enough of squalls. I want placid for a while."

"Eventually, we'll get there, babe. For now, we just have to hold on tight and trust that God will get us through in one piece."

"I know. I just…"

"What?"

"Like to have a little more control over things."

"I get that about you."

She laughed, a soft sound that made him want to turn and look at her again. See the laughter as it played across her face. "I guess it's pretty obvious. I don't mean to be difficult—"

"Who said anything about difficult?"

"I'm sure people have thought it."

"People like Brian?" The more he heard the guy's name,

the less he liked him. As a matter of fact, it had been all he could do not to tell the doctor to get lost and stay lost when he'd stopped in to check on Martha at the hospital.

"People. The thing is, I've just learned how important it is to take care of myself and be responsible for my own decisions. Besides my father, I've never had anyone else to lean on. I've never needed anyone else."

"That's admirable, Martha, but sometimes we do need someone to lean on. Sometimes we really can't go it alone."

"Yeah, I think I'm starting to get that." She was silent for a minute, then she shrugged, her arm brushing against his. "I'd still rather do it on my own. It's easier that way."

"It's always easier to guard our hearts than to open them up to pain, but without pain how would we ever know what joy was?" He spoke as he pulled into the hospital parking lot, his gaze scanning cars, probing shadows. The hair on the back of his neck stood on end, his body humming with adrenaline. Johnson was out there somewhere, and Tristan could almost guarantee he was close.

"Do you think he's here?" Martha whispered as if afraid Johnson would hear her.

"Yeah, but don't worry, we're ready for him." Dozens of officers and agents were stationed around the hospital, ready. Waiting. At least, that was the plan. In all the years he'd worked for the ATF, he'd never doubted that all the players would be in place when a mission began. He trusted his team. But this time, he didn't want to leave things in anyone else's hands.

"Good. Let's get going. As long as we're here, I may as well spend some time with my father." Martha didn't seem at all worried to be stepping out of the car and into danger, and Tristan leaned in, staring into her eyes and trying to convey the seriousness of the situation.

"For someone who may be about to walk into a gunfight, you seem awfully calm, Sunshine."

"Calm? I'm scared out of my mind."

"Good. That'll keep you safe."

"It doesn't feel good. Now, let's get out of here before I chicken out and decide I'd rather not be shark bait." She put her hand on the door handle, but he grabbed her arm, stopping her before she could push it open.

"Wait until I come around."

"Okay."

"And remember, whatever I tell you—"

"Do it. No questions asked. No arguments."

"You know, Sunshine, I think you're finally getting the hang of things." He chucked her under the chin, meaning the gesture to be friendly, brotherly, encouraging. Somehow his hand lingered, his fingers caressing the soft skin beneath her jaw, circling around of their own accord until he was cupping her neck, pulling her in close.

Chocolate. Sunshine. Sweet summer and cool calm fall.

They enveloped him, tempted him.

Her eyes widened, but she didn't pull away as he did what he knew he shouldn't and kissed her. It didn't matter that a handful of police officers and federal agents were watching. It didn't matter that Gordon Johnson might be lurking nearby. It didn't even matter that Tristan had told himself he could never offer a woman the kind of stable life she deserved.

What mattered was seizing the moment, knowing that the moment was all they might have.

Finally, he backed away, catching his breath, wondering when he'd lost his mind to this woman. Or maybe it wasn't his mind he'd lost at all. Maybe it was his heart.

She blinked, put a hand to her lips. "I don't think you should have done that."

"No? I guess we can debate that later. Right now, I need to get you inside that hospital in one piece. Ready?"

"As I'll ever be."

"Then let's do it." He stepped out of the car, letting the cold air slap some sense into him as he pulled Martha's door open and helped her out, shielding her body the best he could, knowing that might not be good enough. His nerves were alive, every sense heightened as he waited for the first bullet to fly. It never did. They stepped across the parking lot, moved toward the hospital doors. No one else approached. No patients. No visitors. At three-thirty in the morning, the hospital was eerily silent. Unnaturally silent. As if it were holding its breath and waiting.

A hundred yards. Fifty. Martha's feet padded against the ground, and Tristan was sure he could hear her teeth chattering, but she continued walking.

Thirty yards. If Johnson planned to make a move, he'd do it soon or he wouldn't do it at all.

Okay, Lord, it's in Your hands. Let us get this guy tonight, before he hurts anyone else. And keep Martha safe through it all. Preserve her life so that she may continue to serve You.

The prayer raced through his mind as he led Martha closer to the doors, and he could almost picture it rising on the cold night air, flying to the heavens on wings of faith. God knew what would happen in the next few hours. He'd work His will out in the way He'd predestined before time began. Tristan believed that, had always believed it. That's what kept him going even when evil seemed to prevail. It's what motivated him, spurred him on. Darkness lived in the world, but would never overcome it. Christ, the great overcomer, had already won the war. People like Gordon Johnson just hadn't realized it yet.

Lord willing, tonight one more bad guy would realize the futility of fighting a battle that had already been lost.

TWENTY-THREE

Nothing happened.

Martha expected it to. She almost hoped it would. If it meant getting Gordon Johnson off the streets and ending her nightmare, she was willing to walk through a hailstorm of bullets. Hopefully the vest she wore would keep her alive during the onslaught.

But Johnson didn't fire. Not even one shot, and before Martha could hyperventilate from anticipation and fear, she and Tristan were in the warm quiet of the hospital lobby.

"That didn't go well." She spoke more to herself than to Tristan, but he responded anyway, taking her arm and leading her to the bank of elevators that lined one wall.

"Or it went very well, depending on your perspective."

"He's still out there somewhere."

"And you're still alive. I'm more than willing to trade one for the other."

"Did you really think he might succeed in killing me?"

"If I did, I would have done what I wanted to—taken the next road to nowhere and helped you disappear."

"You're not serious. You'd lose your job for that."

"And?" He turned to her as the elevator doors closed, his eyes blazing from his hard face.

"I wouldn't want you to lose your job for helping me."

"I wouldn't want you to lose your life so I could keep my job. If that meant kidnapping you and taking you somewhere safe, that's what I'd do."

"You weren't really thinking about kidnapping me?"

"I was." He meant it. The truth was in his eyes and in the intensity of his gaze.

"That would not have been a good idea." But it was an intriguing one. Going off to some unknown destination with a man determined to protect her. A fairy tale come to life. Only this wasn't a fairy tale and the chance of a happy ending was slim to none. "I guess we'll just have to be thankful it didn't come down to that."

"I don't know, Sunshine. I don't think I'd mind spending a few weeks in an exotic location keeping an eye on you."

Her cheeks heated at his words, and he grinned, the flirty mischief in his gaze enough to make her pulse race. She really needed to get a grip. She really needed to focus. Someone wanted her dead and she was mooning over an ATF agent she'd known for less than a week. The door to the elevator slid open and she rushed out into the hall, nearly falling backward as Tristan yanked her to a stop.

"Let me lead, okay?" All the humor was gone from his face and from his eyes. In its place was grim determination and the hard, implacable expression she'd seen at the cabin in the mountains.

"There's no way Gordon could be in here. There are police officers stationed all over this wing. It's impossible."

"I've seen the impossible happen more times than I'd care to remember. Besides, someone called from the hospital. That person may or not be dangerous to you." He led her to the nurses' station, the quiet of the ICU broken by the beep and hum of machinery that supported the lives of the patients there. Tristan spoke to the nurse on duty, but his words didn't register. Martha's heart was beating too hard and too fast, her blood sloshing in her ears.

No matter how many times she told herself not to be afraid, she was. The terror clawed at her, threatening to turn her into a blubbering mass of hysteria if she let it. She was not going to let it. She'd held herself together this long, she was not going to fall apart now.

Keep telling yourself that, Martha. Eventually your racing heart might believe it.

She frowned as Tristan stopped in her father's doorway. "What's wrong?"

"Just making sure nothing is out of place."

"Out of place? There's nothing in there but my dad and a bunch of machines."

"Exactly. So if there is something else lying around—a box, a bag, a duffel—it would be worth checking out."

"A bomb?" She whispered the words as if that could make them less real.

"I doubt it, but it's always better to be cautious." He moved silently, making a circuit of the room, glancing behind machines, under the bed, behind the door. Then, finally, gestured for her to enter. "It's okay. Come on in."

Relieved, she hurried to her father's side. There was some color in his cheeks now, but he still looked awful—tubes and wires snaking out from his mouth, his nose, his chest. "You look like the Bionic Man before he got all his new parts, Dad. Remember how we used to watch that show together while we worked in the store? You had that little black-and-white television, and we'd sit in front of it, watching until a customer came in. Then we'd argue over who was going to ring up the order. You always won, and I always ended up missing half the program." She squeezed his hand, was surprised to feel the pressure returned. "You can hear me, huh?"

He opened his eyes, tried to nod.

"You're supposed to be sleeping."

He gestured for the pad and pen, and scribbled a note. *Better-looking than the Bionic Man. Was sleeping until you came in and woke me.*

Martha laughed. This was her father. Funny. Tough. And she knew in that moment that he was going to make it. "Glad to have you back."

Won't be back until the lung is healed. But getting there.

"Get there fast, because I'm counting on you being out of the hospital by Thanksgiving. Sue puts on a great spread, and I wouldn't want her too distracted to cook."

Thanksgiving. The four of us. It's a date.

"Four?"

Her father's gaze jumped to Tristan who'd moved up beside Martha.

"I'm sure Tristan has plans with his family."

"Do I? And here I was thinking I had plans with *your* family. Now that I'm thinking about it, we could invite the whole clan to my brother Grayson's house. My folks, my siblings, your family. It's the perfect time for everyone to meet." Tristan smiled, and Martha's heart did its crazy little dance again.

"Meet?"

"Sure. If you can survive being stalked by Gordon Johnson, you can survive meeting my family."

"But—"

"I've already met yours, Sunshine. So I'm at an unfair advantage. Once you meet my family, that'll put things on more even footing."

"What things?"

Jesse scribbled on his pad, motioned for Tristan to take it. He read the words, laughing as he met Martha's eyes. "Your dad says I'm going to have my hands full with you."

"I…" She shook her head and gave up. What was the sense in arguing with the two of them? There was no way she could win. "Fine. We'll do Thanksgiving your way if Dad is out of the hospital."

"So you've got plenty of incentive to get better, Jesse." Tristan placed the paper back on the bedside table and took Martha's arm. "To that end, I think our ten minutes are up. I'll bring Martha back as soon as it's possible."

Jesse nodded, his sharp gaze sending a silent message that Martha couldn't decipher. Tristan seemed to understand it. He nodded, patting her dad's hand. "We'll talk more when you're feeling better."

Talk more? About what?

Honestly, it was like they were planning a siege, and she was the enemy. Or maybe she was the princess standing on the other side of the city wall they wanted to batter down.

Either way, she didn't like it.

She waited until they were out of her father's hearing, before turning on Tristan. "Look, I don't know what you and my father are planning, but I don't like it."

"How do you know you don't like it if you don't know what it is?"

"Because it involves talking about me, and I don't like the idea of you two plotting things I don't know about."

"Trust me, Martha, what we're plotting is something you know about." He smiled, but his eyes burned into hers, intense, probing.

She knew, all right. Knew enough to turn tail and run as

soon as she got the opportunity. Tristan was a great guy, but he wasn't the right guy for her. No one was. She'd already decided she was going to be the neighborhood cat lady. No strong, determined, compassionate, good-looking hero was going to change her mind.

She'd forgotten to say "kind." Tristan was that. And loyal, faithful, moral: an all-around good guy. The kind of guy that was hard to come by in this day and age. The kind of guy any woman would be beating down doors to have interested in her.

But Martha wasn't any woman.

She'd learned young that relationships couldn't last. She'd still tried to make it work with Brian. Thank goodness that had ended before they'd taken vows. For better, for worse, in sickness and health. Brian hadn't been able to be with her in the *good* times. There was no way she'd have ever been able to count on him in the bad ones.

Tristan, on the other hand, had only ever been with her in bad times. When good times came, he'd probably move on to the next distressed damsel, the next battle against evil. Not because he'd want to hurt Martha, but because it was what he did. He was one of those rare people who gave everything to others. His passion was for justice. She doubted there could be room for much else. The thought was a lot more depressing than it should have been, and Martha shoved it aside as Tristan led her back outside.

The moon had set and stars dotted the black sky—a field of wishes waiting to be harvested. Martha imagined reaching up, pulling one toward her, reciting that childhood rhyme her father had taught her. Star light, star bright, first star I see tonight, I wish I may, I wish I might, have the wish I wish tonight. What would her wish be? That her father get better quickly? That her life go back to normal?

That Tristan stay?

It didn't matter. Wishes were only hopes given voice, they had no power. Power lay with God, and only He could fulfill the desires of the heart.

Soon this would be over. She'd go back to her life. Tristan would go back to his. The world would right itself again, and she'd find her balance. Then she'd look back and laugh at how her heart had seemed to beat in time with Tristan's, at how her pulse raced when she looked into his eyes. At how much she seemed to belong when she was with him.

Tristan pulled the car door open, his hand on her waist, steadying her as she slid inside. "Buckle up, this could be a wild ride."

"A wild ride? I thought the worst was over."

"It may be, but Johnson isn't one to give up. He was too smart to try anything here, and smart enough to know that we're most vulnerable when we're on the road. If we leave here without an escort, he just might make his move."

"So we're on our own from here on out?"

"We're never on our own, babe."

"I know, but I'd feel a little better if we had some tangible proof of God's protection. Like maybe an armored car, or a military escort."

"We've got backup standing by in various locations on our route. It'll be okay."

"For someone who thinks that, you sure don't look happy."

"I'm never happy when I'm dragging an innocent person into something dangerous. The fact that it's you I'm dragging only makes it worse."

"You still have to do your job. It's who you are."

"You're right about that, babe. I have to do it, but I don't have to like it." Grim faced, he started the car and pulled out of the parking lot, leaving the relative safety of the hospital behind them.

They drove in silence. No radio. No conversation. Tristan's tension filled the car, and Martha's joined it, welling up and out until it seemed to steal the oxygen. She took a deep, shaky breath, forcing herself to relax.

Five minutes passed. Then ten. Cars and trucks passed them on their way into the Blue Ridge Mountains. Despite the hour, the road was busy, and Martha started to relax. To believe that Johnson had given up, that he'd decided killing her wasn't worth taking a chance. Tristan wound his way up into the mountains, leaving Lynchburg behind, the sheer drop below shrouded by darkness.

Ten minutes. The traffic thinned a little as they drove along Blue Ridge Parkway, but was still heavy enough that Martha felt confident Johnson wouldn't strike. Five more minutes and they'd reach the turnoff that led to the safe house.

"Here he comes."

"What? How do you—" Before she could finish, they were hit from behind. The sedan slid sideways toward a sheer drop.

Martha screamed, her hands clutching the dashboard as she imagined plummeting a hundred feet to the ground below. She'd always loved the Blue Ridge Parkway, but if she made it off this road alive, she would never, ever drive on it again.

Tristan righted the wheels, stepping on the accelerator and racing ahead of the vehicle behind them. Fifty miles an hour. Sixty. Seventy. Eighty. Martha's heart beat so hard, she thought it would jump out of her chest. Johnson wasn't going to have to hit them again, they were going to lose control and die without any help from him at all.

"Hang on." Tristan took a corner so fast, Martha's head slammed into the side window and she saw stars. When she could see again, she realized they were on a dirt road rather than the gravel road that led to the safe house. Not where they should be, but at least they weren't racing along a sheer drop.

Tristan eased his foot from the accelerator, his speed dropping to thirty. Martha barely had time to thank God for that, when they were hit again, this time with more force. The car spun off the road, tumbling sideways, sliding into trees. Snapping. Crashing. Crunching. Glass shattering. Air bags popping. Blood. Pain.

Silence as still as death.

Not a breath. Not a sound.

She wanted to believe it was over. Wanted to think it was the end, but her heart knew the truth. Gordon Johnson was right outside the car, and any minute he'd pull open her door and finish what he'd started.

"You okay?" Tristan pressed a palm against her cheek, and she nodded, wanting to press her hand over his, force him to maintain contact, but her arm wouldn't listen to the command her brain issued. "Good. I tried to slow down to keep the damage at a minimum, but he was still coming fast."

"Is he out there?"

"Oh, yeah, he's out there. And he and I are about to have a little face-to-face." His hand dropped away, and this time Martha managed to grab it.

"You can't go out there."

"Sure I can. It's what I'm trained to do."

"But he's got a gun."

"Yeah? So do I."

"So let's wait longer. Eventually, your backup will arrive. They can take care of Johnson."

"That's not how it works, Sunshine. I've got our perp close enough to take down. I'm not going to risk letting him get away."

"But—"

"We rolled down a slope and through some thick foliage. It's going to take a little time for him to get down here. You stay put while I go find him."

"Tristan, I really don't like this plan."

"I know, but you've got to trust me on this, babe. It's the only way. Stay here." His voice had softened, and his fingers skimmed across her brow, down her cheek, touching her lips briefly before slipping away. "Promise me, Sunshine. No matter what, you won't get out of this car. You've got to trust me to take care of this situation."

"I can't."

"Then I can't go looking for Johnson. I won't leave you here knowing you might walk right into danger." He was serious. He really wasn't going to leave. Martha sensed it in the stiff way he settled back into his seat, the tense way he held his body.

"Go. I'll stay here."

"Promise." It was a demand rather than a request, but Martha couldn't deny it. Couldn't deny who Tristan was, or ask him to do it. He was meant for this job. No matter what, she had to trust him and let him do it.

"I promise."

He leaned in, and she could smell soap and shampoo and autumn cold as he pressed his lips to her forehead. "Don't take this the wrong way, babe, but I think I'm falling for you."

Then he was gone, sliding out the window and into the predawn, not even a rustle of leaves letting her know which direction he'd gone.

And Martha was alone. A sitting duck waiting for a wolf to move in for the kill.

TWENTY-FOUR

At first all she could hear was her rushing pulse, but as minutes passed and nothing happened, she began to hear other things. Leaves whispering. The first bright trills of a songbird. Cars somewhere in the distance. Life going on while she sat and waited for death.

Well, she was done waiting. Gordon Johnson might want her dead, but that didn't mean she had to make it easy for him. She slid across the seat, her head butting against the crushed roof, her arm throbbing with a deep insistent pain that was nearly impossible to ignore.

It didn't matter. All that mattered was sliding out of the window, fading into the shadows and finding a place to hide from the Grim Reaper. She shifted her weight, almost had her head out the window, when she heard Tristan's words, clear as a bell ringing in her ears. A memory, but so vivid she could almost believe he was beside her again. "Promise me, Sunshine. No matter what, you won't get out of this car. You've got to trust me to take care of this situation."

And then, whisper soft, echoing in her heart—"don't take this the wrong way, babe, but I think I'm falling for you."

Falling for her.

With those simple words, he'd tied her hands. Made her a

prisoner to her promise. She couldn't betray a man who believed in her, who was counting on her. If she got out of the car and put Tristan in danger, she'd never forgive herself.

She sank back into the car, tears streaming down her cheeks. Helpless. Angry. But more than that, afraid. Afraid that everything she'd ever wanted had just stepped out into the darkness and she'd been too foolish to believe in it, too cowardly to go after it.

"Lord, please keep Tristan safe. Keep me safe. I realize now the gift that You've given me. I realize now that I can't be too afraid to take it. Please, let everything turn out okay."

Branches cracked nearby. Heavy footfalls. A muffled curse. Not Tristan. Gordon Johnson. She didn't need to see his face to picture him. Red hair. Pale eyes. Death in his cold, unfeeling gaze.

She shuddered, her mind screaming for her to run, to slide out the window and take off before Johnson found her. Her heart wouldn't let her do it.

Her treacherous, traitorous heart.

The one that refused to believe in love.

The one that insisted fairy tales were nothing more than fantasy.

The one that had already created a neighborhood cat-lady existence for herself, wouldn't let her betray Tristan or his trust in her.

So she waited, as the footfalls grew nearer, the curses grew louder, until finally, branches were pulled away from the car, and Gordon Johnson was inches from her face.

"Where's your friend?" He growled the question, turning to the left, then the right, a gun in his hand. Not the gun he'd had in the mountains. A different gun. One with a silencer.

Lord, please, please let Tristan be around. I don't want to die. I really, really don't.

"I'm alone." She managed to squeak the word out as her mind made plans for escape. Not that she'd get far before Johnson put a bullet in her back, but if she was going down, she was going down fighting.

"You're not alone. You got a friend with you. He was driving. And I'm thinking it might be my old buddy Sky Davis, so tell me where he is now, and I can finish my business with you and be on my way."

"I said—"

He lifted the gun, pointed it at her forehead, and she knew she was going to die. Knew it in the deepest part of her soul. No husband. No kids. Not even any cats. If she hadn't been so scared she would have cried, maybe even begged for her life.

"Looking for me?" Tristan's voice came from out of the darkness, and Johnson whirled toward the sound.

"Come on out here where I can see you, Davis. I got a score to settle with you. I gave you my trust. You repaid me with a betrayal."

"You're scum, Gordon. A lackey working for someone else because you don't have the brains to do the job yourself."

"I got news for you, Davis. I'm not the one sitting behind bars. Buddy is. So, who's the one with less brains?"

"I'd say neither of you have much, because you're going to be joining your boss soon."

"Not if I have anything to say about it." Johnson fired a shot, a pop and a flash of light that disappeared almost before Martha could see it.

Her heart jumped, her stomach churning. Where was Tristan's backup? Where was the cavalry? Shouldn't someone be riding to the rescue by now?

"Put the gun down, Gordon. You've lost this battle. You'll get to fight another one in court."

"You're wrong, Davis. I haven't lost anything." He grabbed Martha's hair, pulling her halfway out of the car. "Come on out now, before I make hamburger out of your girlfriend's face." Johnson lifted the gun, aimed it at Martha's face while she struggled against his iron grip on her hair.

Would it be quick?

Would she feel anything?

Was God already opening His arms to welcome her home?

The thoughts hammered through her mind, beating with the loud, horrifying thump of her heart.

No. Tristan wasn't going to let her die. He was going to—

A loud crack split the silence, and Johnson cursed, his grip on her hair going lax. She scrambled back, away from the shattered window and the killer outside. Her fingers clawing at the far door, her shoulder slamming into it as she tried to get it open.

Stuck tight.

Her breath heaved out in great, gasping sobs as branches cracked, sirens blared, men shouted and the world spun crazily in its orbit.

A dark shadow loomed in front of her, and Martha screamed, lurching back.

"Hey, it's okay." Tristan yanked hard on the crushed door, pulling it open and climbing into the car, enveloping her in his strength.

She wrapped her arms around him, her fingers fisted in his shirt. "I've never been so scared in my life."

"Me neither. I thought I was going to lose you before I ever even had you." His voice was steady, but his heart was racing wildly against her ear.

"Is Johnson—"

"Alive. Justice is better served that way."

"But you did shoot him?"

"His arm. Paramedics are already treating him. Come on. Let's get you out of here."

He started to move away, but Martha tightened her grip. "I don't think I can move. My legs aren't working. Can we sit for a little while longer?"

"We can sit for as long as you want."

"Don't say that. I might stay here forever."

"From where I'm sitting, that doesn't seem like such a bad thing." She could feel his smile against her hair, feel his heart slowing and her heart responding. Her pulse eased, her breathing calmed, her tense muscles relaxed as if they knew the truth she hadn't wanted to accept—that Tristan was exactly what she'd always been looking for. Home. Belonging. Family.

She sighed, wishing she *could* stay there with him forever, cocooned in his arms, and forget everything but this moment. Good things never lasted and tomorrow Tristan might be gone.

Outside the car, men and women called to each other, flashlights danced along the ground. A cool breeze blew moisture through the trees. Twenty miles away, her father lay in intensive care, struggling to survive.

And Martha knew she needed to step back into the world again. She loosened her grip on Tristan and leaned back, putting some distance between them. "I guess I can go to the hospital and be with my father now."

"I guess you can."

"And I guess you won't be needing that apartment over my garage anymore."

"I guess not."

"So, I guess this is probably goodbye."

He chuckled, shook his head. "Haven't you been listening to a word I've said, Sunshine? I'm not going anywhere."

"But it's over. I'm safe."

"So we've made it through the bad times together. How about we start making it through some good times?"

"Like Thanksgiving with both families?"

"For a start."

"What if your family doesn't like me?"

"Grayson likes you. If you meet with his approval, you're a shoo-in with everyone else. Besides, I'm past the age where I need my family's approval."

"What if you decide I'm too stubborn for my own good and get sick of being around me?"

"What if you decide my job takes me away too much and you get tired of having me gone?"

"Your job is what you're meant to do, Tristan. I would never resent you for that."

"And your determination is what makes you a strong, independent woman. The way I see it, if anyone can handle being with someone whose job takes him away more than he's home, you can."

"So we're on for Thanksgiving?"

"And for painting my parents' house, if you're up to it."

"Painting their house?"

"Yep. An old Victorian lady that gets her hair and nails done the first weekend in November every three years. We can always use an extra set of hands. And don't think you'll get out of painting because you've been shot. It's all hands on deck when it comes to the job."

"It sounds like..." Like fun, like family, like everything she'd dreamed of when she was a kid.

"Like what?"

"Like good times."

"Then it's a date?" He held out his hand, and she took a deep breath, then did what her heart was telling her to, and took it.

"It's a date."

Tristan's smile warmed her as he tugged her out of the car.

EPILOGUE

"You missed a spot." Martha couldn't hide her smile as Tristan glanced down from the scaffold he was perched on. A paintbrush in his good hand, a scowl on his face, he looked like a knight braced for battle rather than a man painting a three-story Victorian monstrosity.

Her knight.

She smiled again.

Being independent and capable was great. She highly recommended it, but she had to admit, being cherished and taken care of wasn't such a bad thing either. Especially when the guy doing the cherishing was Tristan.

"Did one of my brothers send you over here to tell me that? Because if it was Grayson—"

"Actually, I discovered the problem all by myself."

"Did you? Well, far be it from me to do a less than perfect job. Come on up here and tell me where it is, and I'll fix the problem. For a price."

"A price?"

"A kiss. Or two." He grinned, and Martha's heart jumped in response.

No matter how many times she looked into his eyes, no matter how many smiles they shared, how much laughter passed between them, it always felt like the best of surprises; the most wonderful of gifts.

"I'd love to, but your father expressly forbid me to climb up any ladders for fear that I'd reinjure my shoulder."

"Funny, he didn't seem nearly as concerned about my injury. As a matter of fact, he told me I'd better not think I could slack off because of a little gunshot wound."

"Then maybe you shouldn't have told him *I* couldn't paint."

"Piper's been talking to you, hasn't she? Why won't she just have the kid already so she can stop causing trouble?" He smiled as he said it, and Martha laughed, moving closer as Tristan climbed down from the scaffold.

"I like your family."

"I knew you would."

"I especially like them because they're not making *me* paint."

"Keep it up, Sunshine, and I'll tell your dad you're not treating me right."

"You may be his favorite son, but I'm still his little princess. Your whining won't do any good."

"Brat."

She laughed again, and he pressed his lips to hers, drinking in her joy, sharing it with her.

Breathless, she stepped back. "We're really going to make this work, aren't we?"

"This, as in you and me?"

"What else?"

"Yeah, Sunshine, we really are."

"You know, just a few short weeks ago, I was sure I'd wind up being the neighborhood cat lady. You know the one. Tucked away in her house with twenty cats and no friends, overgrown bushes blocking out the sunlight."

"I couldn't imagine that happening to you even if I tried."

He brushed stray curls from her cheek, his eyes the deep blue of summer sunsets.

"That's because you see something in me no one else ever has."

"It's because I see *you*. The person God created. Sweet and gentle, but with a spine of steel. You were meant to have a family, Martha."

"Maybe, but I'm scared."

"Of me?"

"Of *me*. What if I'm like my mother? What if, as soon as things get tough, I take off running? What if we create something really good together and I mess it up?"

"You've got too much love in you to ever do that."

"But—"

"You worry too much, you know that?"

"I just don't want to be disappointed."

"I will never disappoint you, Sunshine. And you'll never disappoint yourself. God planned this out from the very beginning. From the moment you walked into the cabin in the mountains, I knew there would be something between us. I felt it in my soul. We were meant to meet that day. We're meant to be together now. We're meant to have a future together. I believe that or I wouldn't be standing here with you now." He stared into her eyes as if he could will his confidence into her.

But he didn't need to.

She felt it. Just as he'd said. Deep inside, where the quiet voice of the Spirit whispered truth. Where God spoke to her heart, telling her that He'd planned it all before her life began. "You know what?" She pulled his head down for a kiss. "I believe it, too."

"That is exactly what I was hoping to hear." He claimed

her lips again, pulling her in, promising her what she'd always longed for and had been so afraid she'd never have.

"Hey! I'm hard at work on the west side and I come over here and find my brother being distracted by one of the prettiest women in the house. That doesn't seem right." Grayson's voice cut through the haze of Martha's emotions, and she jerked back, her cheeks heating as Tristan chuckled.

"You're just jealous."

"Jealous that you're succumbing to the love bug? I don't think so. I've been there. Done that. As far as I'm concerned, that's enough for one lifetime." He turned away, calling over his shoulder as he went. "Mom just told me lunch is on the table. You're welcome to stay out here as long as you want, but don't expect me to save you any of the good stuff. And that includes the cherry cobbler she made."

"We'd better hurry." Martha started after Grayson, but Tristan pulled her up short.

"Let's take our time. The way I see it, I've got something a lot sweeter than Mom's cherry cobbler right here beside me." His eyes were filled with humor, his stride easy as he wrapped his arm around Martha's waist and led her into their future.

* * * * *

Dear Reader,

Life is filled with choices. When we take time to pray and seek God's will, we have peace that comes from knowing we're walking in God's will. When we don't, we find ourselves at crossroads, unsure of which direction to go. Martha Gabler is in just such a place. Desperate to be married, she allows herself to be pulled into a relationship that isn't God's plan. When she finally realizes her mistake, she hikes into the Blue Ridge Mountains, planning to spend time praying about God's will for her life. Instead, she finds danger and intrigue and learns that God's vision for her life is much better than anything she could have imagined or dreamed.

I hope you enjoy Martha's story, and I pray that whatever choices you're faced with, you will find the peace that comes from seeking God's plan for your life.

In Him,

Shirlee McCoy

QUESTIONS FOR DISCUSSION

1. After breaking up with Brian, Martha realizes a relationship with him wasn't the best thing for her. Why doesn't she realize this before becoming engaged to him?

2. How does knowing this make her feel?

3. Have you made decisions that you've convinced yourself were right, then discovered they were mistakes? Why do you think this happened?

4. Martha's childhood impacts the way she looks at the world and at herself. What are her feelings about marriage and motherhood? How do they change over the course of the story?

5. How has your childhood experience impacted your life? How does faith change the way you look at the world?

6. What is Tristan's motivation for going to Lakeview? Does this change during the story?

7. Martha is strong, determined and not necessarily in need of a hero. Somehow, though, Tristan fills a place in her life that's been empty. What is it about Tristan that appeals to Martha?

8. What is it about Martha that Tristan finds attractive?

9. Trusting God isn't always easy for Martha. What is it in her personality that makes sitting back and waiting so hard?

10. Tristan seems like the perfect hero, but Martha doesn't want to believe that he might become something more than that to her. Why?

11. When given a choice between taking action and waiting on God's will, Martha is more likely to act than to wait. Can you identify with this? What things in your life have you had to wait on?

12. It is difficult for Martha to accept help from others. She's been taught to take care of herself. Do you have difficulty accepting help from those around you? How does this affect your life?

13. Vulnerability is often seen as a weakness, but Martha learns that to be strong we must sometimes allow ourselves to be weak. How does being vulnerable before God make us stronger? ·

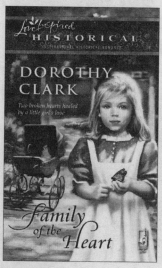

REQUEST YOUR FREE BOOKS!

2 FREE RIVETING INSPIRATIONAL NOVELS
PLUS 2 FREE MYSTERY GIFTS

YES! Please send me 2 FREE Love Inspired® Suspense novels and my 2 FREE mystery gifts (gifts are worth about $10). After receiving them, if I don't wish to receive any more books, I can return the shipping statement marked "cancel". If I don't cancel, I will receive 4 brand-new novels every month and be billed just $4.24 per book in the U.S. or $4.74 per book in Canada, plus 25¢ shipping and handling per book and applicable taxes, if any*. That's a savings of over 20% off the cover price! I understand that accepting the 2 free books and gifts places me under no obligation to buy anything. I can always return a shipment and cancel at any time. Even if I never buy another book, the two free books and gifts are mine to keep forever.

123 IDN ERXX 323 IDN ERXM

Name	(PLEASE PRINT)
Address	Apt. #
City	State/Prov.	Zip/Postal Code

Signature (if under 18, a parent or guardian must sign)

Order online at www.LoveInspiredSuspense.com
Or mail to Steeple Hill Reader Service:

IN U.S.A.: P.O. Box 1867, Buffalo, NY 14240-1867
IN CANADA: P.O. Box 609, Fort Erie, Ontario L2A 5X3

Not valid to current subscribers of Love Inspired Suspense books.

Want to try two free books from another series?
Call 1-800-873-8635 or visit www.morefreebooks.com

* Terms and prices subject to change without notice. N.Y. residents add applicable sales tax. Canadian residents will be charged applicable provincial taxes and GST. Offer not valid in Quebec. This offer is limited to one order per household. All orders subject to approval. Credit or debit balances in a customer's account(s) may be offset by any other outstanding balance owed by or to the customer. Please allow 4 to 6 weeks for delivery. Offer available while quantities last.

Your Privacy: Steeple Hill Books is committed to protecting your privacy. Our Privacy Policy is available online at www.SteepleHill.com or upon request from the Reader Service. From time to time we make our lists of customers available to reputable third parties who have a product or service of interest to you. If you would prefer we not share your name and address, please check here. ☐

LISUS08R

Love Inspired

Only one person knows why Kat Thatcher left her Oklahoma hometown ten years ago. That person is Seth Washington. And now that she's back, he's only too available to talk about the past. Seth insists the Lord is on their side and always was. But will that be enough for love?

Look for

A Time To Heal

by

Linda Goodnight

Steeple Hill®

LI87497

Love Inspired ®
SUSPENSE

TITLES AVAILABLE NEXT MONTH

Don't miss these four stories in September

DOUBLE CROSS by Terri Reed
The McClains
Her family's orchid farm is Kiki Brill's pride and joy. She won't sell, no matter how much Ryan McClain offers. But as accidents threaten her peaceful life on Maui, the wealthy, handsome businessman, once the prime suspect, begins to seem like her last hope.

BADGE OF HONOR by Carol Steward
In the Line of Fire
Why would FBI agent Sarah Roberts start over as a small-town cop? She *has* to be undercover. And police officer Nick Matthews knows exactly who Sarah is spying on: him. Then Sarah's past crashes down on them. Trusting his new partner becomes a matter of life, death—and love.

THE FACE OF DECEIT by Ramona Richards
Karen O'Neill barely remembers her parents' murder. Still, she's haunted by a face—which she sculpts into her vases. Now, an art buyer is dead and Karen's vases are being shattered. Art expert Mason DuBroc believes the clues are in the clay. Can they decode them in time?

FINAL DEPOSIT by Lisa Harris
It's bad enough that Lindsey Taylor's father lost his savings in an Internet scam. Now he's gone to claim his "fortune," and Lindsey fears she'll never see him again. Financial security expert Kyle Walker promises to help her. But the closer they get, the more danger they find....

LISCNM0808